sleuth  or dare

Sleepover Stakeout

sleuth or dare

sleuth or dare

Sleepover Stakeout

Kim Harrington

Scholastic Inc.

NEW YORK   TORONTO   LONDON   AUCKLAND

SYDNEY   MEXICO CITY   NEW DELHI   HONG KONG

No part of this work may be reproduced, stored in a retrieval system, or transmitted in any form or by any means, electronic, mechanical, photocopying, recording, or otherwise, without written permission of the publisher. For information regarding permission, write to Scholastic Inc., Attention: Permissions Department, 557 Broadway, New York, NY 10012.

ISBN 978-0-545-38965-5

12 11 10 9 8 7 6 5 4 3 2 1   12 13 14 15 16 17/0

Printed in the U.S.A.   40
First edition, June 2012

Book design by Tim Hall

sleuth or dare

Sleepover Stakeout

Chapter 1

"The pizza is frozen," Fiona said, her green eyes shimmering with excitement. "I repeat . . . the pizza is frozen!"

Darcy and I exchanged confused glances. "What are you talking about?" Darcy asked Fiona. "What pizza?"

Fiona nodded at the cell phone in her hand. "You know . . . the *thing*. I was using code to tell you it's not moving yet."

Darcy rolled her eyes. "We don't need code words. It's just me, you, and Norah here."

Darcy was right. It *was* only the three of us: me, Norah Burridge; my best friend, Darcy Carter; and our other friend, Fiona Fanning. We were the members of

1

Partners in Crime, a detective agency Darcy and I had started just a few weeks ago.

Now we were huddled against the brick back wall of Danville Middle School. It was Friday afternoon, so most kids had already left, but we were sticking around.

We were undercover.

Our classmate Abigail Mattimore had e-mailed us through the Partners in Crime website. She had a raging crush on Trey Watson, a popular jock in our grade, and she thought he might like her, too. They'd been talking and texting a lot. But every Friday afternoon, he disappeared. He would never answer his phone or say where he was. Abigail had his whole schedule memorized (stalker alert!) and knew he had no sports practice. She was worried that he was meeting another girl on Fridays. I suggested she just ask him, but Abigail said she didn't want to seem crazy.

Yet, somehow, hiring a detective agency run by seventh graders *wasn't* nuts.

So we took on the case and were now staking out Trey. Fiona's parents had a GPS on her cell phone that tracked where she was at all times. She thought it was annoying and overprotective, but it was sure coming in handy solving this mystery. Fiona had "accidentally" dropped her phone into Trey's backpack near the end of the school day. Now all we had to do was wait. We were tracking its signal on an app on Darcy's phone. As soon as the signal started moving, we'd know Trey was heading to his secret place.

And, according to Fiona's pizza code — it was standing still for now, meaning Trey was still in school.

It was kind of funny seeing Fiona all into being a detective with us. Only a month ago, I never would have pictured even being friends with her. Fiona is the prettiest, most popular girl in our school. Darcy and I are nerds and proud of it. Usually those two worlds don't mix, but we were enjoying sleuthing together.

"Let her use the code if she wants," I said to Darcy.

"Oh, fine," Darcy said, tucking a purple-striped chunk of her short black hair behind her ear.

Fiona took a moment to eyeball my T-shirt. I'm not into fashion like she is, but this was my favorite item of clothing. It's a shirt I got at the Museum of Science that says "Pluto: Revolve in Peace 1930–2006."

"What does that mean?" Fiona said, frowning. Her long brown hair was twisted into this beautiful, complicated updo that I would need a degree in engineering to copy. I always wore my blond hair straight down my back, or up in a plain ponytail.

"It's a joke," I said. "Like 'R.I.P.' but 'revolve' in peace. Get it? Because Pluto was demoted from planet status in 2006 . . ."

"Huh," Fiona said. I'd already lost her.

We each have our own hobbies. I'm an astronomy buff. Fiona is a fashionista. She can't name any of Jupiter's moons, but I don't know any expensive shoe designers, so we're even. Darcy's into technology, crime, and conspiracies, and she's totally obsessed with the TV show *Crime Scene: New York.*

Even though we all have our own interests, we work well together. At least, we have so far. This is only our second case. And we never meant to become private investigators. It started as a class project. But once we solved our first mystery, we were hooked.

"The pizza is on the move!" Fiona yelled. My heart jumped. She passed the cell phone to Darcy. We all huddled around it and watched the little red dot on the GPS map. Once we saw which direction Trey was going, we'd hop on our bikes, catch up, and find out where he went every Friday.

"Wait!" Fiona's voice was panicked. "It's moving too fast."

I squinted at the map. The dot had already left the school parking lot and was headed down Main Street. Definitely too fast to be someone walking. "Is he on a bike?" I asked.

Darcy watched for a moment. "Don't think so. He must be in a car."

"Well, let's motor," I said. "The car has to stop sometime."

We jumped on our bikes. Darcy had the cell in her hand, so she took the lead. Fiona and I followed behind her, pedaling hard. After ten minutes, we stopped in the center of town.

"What's up?" I asked my BFF, panting. "You need a break?"

Darcy frowned at the cell phone. "Nope. It stopped. He's in there." She pointed at a place called the Java Lamp. My mom had mentioned it once or twice as a great new spot to get afternoon lattes.

"A coffee shop?" I said, surprised. I love the smell of coffee, but I don't drink it. First, because I have enough trouble shutting my mind off and falling asleep at night as it is. Second, because I tried it once and it tasted like a cup of melted pennies.

"I guess Abigail was right," Darcy said. "He *is* meeting someone else."

Dread formed in the pit of my stomach, but I tried to remain hopeful. After all, Trey *had* come in a car. Maybe it was a family tradition or something. Coffee Fridays! Okay, even I wasn't believing that.

I sighed, then looked at my friends. "Let's go get the evidence." All we needed was for Darcy to snap a picture with her cell phone and e-mail it to Abigail, and the case would be over.

And Abigail's heart would be broken.

I thought about *my* crush, Zane Munro, and how I would feel if he was meeting a girl every Friday at the Java Lamp. A girl who wasn't me. At the mere thought of it, my heart cinched.

I wished it didn't have to end this way for Abigail. Man, being a private investigator was tough.

Darcy shoved open the door with one shoulder, and Fiona and I followed her in. The place was packed. A big red lava lamp bubbled over the cash register. Little round tables were full of people holding steaming coffee mugs, chatting, reading books, or pretending to work on their laptops while eavesdropping on the table of women next to them. (Okay, that last one might have been just one guy.)

Trey, however, was nowhere to be seen.

"Maybe he's in the bathroom," I said.

Darcy made a beeline for a glass case that held baked goods. "You guys!" she called, waving us over. "They have giant cookies! They're the size of my face!"

Fiona ignored her. She was too busy checking out a table of cute boys. Was I the only one who remembered what we were here for?

Just then, an employee wearing a Java Lamp apron went up on the empty stage in the corner and turned on the microphone. Feedback screeched through the room, and people clapped their hands over their ears.

"Testing one, two, three. Sorry about that, folks," he said. "We're happy to have one of our favorites return this afternoon to do a few songs for us."

An afternoon with flavored coffee, giant cookies, and live music . . . how romantic for Trey and his girl.

I was suddenly starting to get angry for Abigail. Why did he make her think he liked her? I might do more than take a picture. I might give him a piece of my mind.

The man leaned into the mic. "Everyone, please put your hands together for . . . Trey!"

Wait, what? The audience clapped, but I stood still, shocked. Trey — the big tough captain of the lacrosse team — sang on Friday afternoons in a coffeehouse?

Trey walked across the stage, carrying a guitar and looking uncharacteristically shy. He wrapped his hand around the microphone and spoke in a soft voice. "This one's for Abigail. Maybe someday I'll be brave enough to invite her here to listen."

Darcy, Fiona, and I all exchanged stunned glances. We could only watch, mouths agape, as Trey sang a sweet song about crushing on a girl. A woman in the front row clapped the loudest. She had Trey's dark hair and blue eyes, so she was clearly his mom — and also the person who had driven him here.

Fiona and I joined Darcy at the counter to buy ourselves cookies as rewards. Darcy snapped a picture of Trey playing his guitar, then turned to us. "Good work, guys!" she exclaimed. "Partners in Crime has solved their second case. And I'm sure Abigail will be excited."

Fiona nodded, grinning. "We did it! Code words and all."

I took a giant chomp out of my chocolate-chip cookie. I was happy that the case was closed *and* that Abigail wasn't going to spend the night crying. But I was also a tiny bit aggravated that the whole thing could've been avoided if Abigail and Trey had only talked to each other.

"What's wrong, Norah?" asked Fiona.

I shook my head. "Well, it's just that Trey kept this secret from Abigail. She kept her worries from him. People need to be more honest about their feelings!"

Darcy let out a giant laugh and gave me a look.

"What?" I said indignantly.

She pointed her cookie at me. "You think boys and girls should be honest about their feelings?"

I jutted my chin out. "Yes, I do."

Darcy laughed again. "Two words for you, Norah: Zane Munro."

I blushed. She had me there.

Chapter 2

Monday morning was a disaster.

For some reason, I'd copied down the wrong math assignment off the board on Friday. So instead of doing the problems on page thirty-three, I did all the problems on page thirty-eight. I was totally lost for the first ten minutes of class and spent the rest of the time playing catchup.

Then, on my way out of the classroom, I slipped on a pencil someone had left on the floor, and my books went flying everywhere. Slade Durkin started laughing — way too loud — which made me think he might have been the one who'd "accidentally" left his pencil there to be slipped on. Or he might have just been enjoying my trauma because he's meaner than dirt. (That's actually an insult to dirt. Dirt isn't so bad. Especially when compared to Slade.)

Slade's best friend, Hunter Fisk, came up next to him. They were both in seventh grade but didn't look it. They were already taller than some of the teachers. I half expected them to start shaving any day.

Slade showed Hunter my booksplosion and they slapped high five. Then, as I knelt down and gathered up my things, they walked on by, laughing in the most obnoxious way.

By midday I was glad for a break. I walked into the cafeteria and found Fiona already sitting at our table. Up until recently, lunch had always been just Darcy and me. Fiona's spot was at the center table with the popular crew. But since we'd become friends with her, Fiona sat at our table some days and with the popular kids on other days. It was like a joint custody agreement.

Darcy had been out that morning because she'd had a dentist appointment. But I knew she was due in soon. I laid my paper lunch bag down and Fiona examined my face with her head tilted to the side.

"What?" I asked.

"Your look," she said. "It's missing something, but I don't know what it is."

"Um, designer clothes? Straight-ironed hair? High-lights? Makeup?" All the things that made Fiona so pretty.

Fiona frowned. "Of course not. That's not your style. But you need *something*. I just can't put my finger on it."

She reached out and pulled the elastic from my hair.

"Ouch! What are you doing?"

"Shush. I'm just trying something. Your hair is such a pretty shade of blond."

I stayed completely still while Fiona ruffled my hair and bangs with her fingers. When she was finished, I gave my hair a tentative touch. It felt . . . big and frizzy.

She handed me the elastic. "Nah, put it back up."

I groaned and pulled my hair back into the ponytail.

"I'll figure out what you need," Fiona insisted. "It just hasn't hit me yet."

I didn't doubt that Fiona was a master at this stuff. Her sketchbook was full of totally cute fashion designs. But I lacked that knowledge. That's why I tended to wear jeans most days, while Fiona looked ready for the runway.

I was opening my lunch bag when Fiona looked up and said, "Uh-oh."

Darcy was stomping across the room with her arms crossed tightly. She wore black boots, black tights, a black skirt, a long-sleeved black tee, and her angry face. She wasn't coming from a funeral. That was her typical look. But still, she seemed a bit more disturbed than usual.

"What's up?" I asked when she got to the table.

Darcy slumped into the chair beside me. "The dentist said I need braces."

"Oh no." I patted her shoulder. "I'm sorry." Darcy was addicted to gum and candy, the chewier the better. I wondered if she'd be forced to cut back.

Fiona smiled like one of those models in a teeth-whitening commercial. "It's okay. Like half the kids in our grade have had them."

"*You're* not getting them, Miss Perfect Teeth," Darcy said.

But before Fiona could respond, someone else said, "I had braces. They weren't so bad."

I froze at the sound of his voice. Was this real or just a wonderful dream?

I looked up over my right shoulder. Zane Munro was standing there wearing jeans and his soccer jersey. He was one of the stars of our school's team, but that wasn't why I had a major-league crush on him. It wasn't his cute freckles or his adorably messy brown hair, either. It was that he was cool without even trying. He was nice to everyone. He wasn't a jerk like some other kids in school (coughcoughHunter-andSladecoughcough).

"When did you get your braces off, Zane?" Fiona asked.

"Over the weekend!" He smiled big to show off his braces-less teeth.

I wanted to say he looked great. I tried. My brain sent signals to my mouth to speak, but my voice wouldn't cooperate.

"Looks great!" Fiona said. In a bubbly voice, not a flirty one, thank goodness. Almost every boy at Danville Middle School had a crush on Fiona at some point. She could have them all, as far as I was concerned. Except this one.

"Thanks," Zane replied. "It really wasn't that bad, Darcy. Your teeth are sore for a couple days after the braces get tightened, but that's a good excuse to beg your mom for ice cream."

Darcy grunted in response. I think she just had her mind made up that this was the end of the world and nothing anyone said would change it.

"So, um, Norah?" Zane looked at me.

Is he here to ask me something? Oh my universe, yes, he is going to ask me something!

I tried to talk my face into not turning ten shades of red while I said, "Yeah?"

"I was absent last Friday and we have that big Spanish test next week. I was wondering if I could borrow your notes from Friday's class?"

My heart sank. All he wanted were class notes?

"Yeah, sure." I reached down into my backpack, pulled out my green notebook, and handed it to him. "Here you go. Just try to get it back to me by sixth period."

"Oh. I didn't realize you'd have it with you now." He took the notebook, then gave a little wave. "'Bye, guys."

I turned back to my sandwich, a little depressed, but Fiona and Darcy were staring at me. "What?" I said. Did I have something in my teeth?

"He totally likes you!" Fiona said.

I wish, but no. "All he wanted were my notes, Fiona."

"He could have asked anyone for those notes," she pointed out. "He has friends in class. Why didn't he ask one of them?"

I shrugged. "Because I'm a nerd and take great notes."

Darcy said, "If that was the case, he could've asked any nerd. He could've asked me."

I didn't want to explain to Miss Grumpy Pants that in her current mood, no one would ask her for anything.

"I think he was using the notes as an excuse to talk to you," Fiona said, twirling a long strand of brown hair around her finger. "He seemed disappointed when you had the notebook right here. Like he was hoping you'd have to meet up at your locker or even after school or something."

I shook my head. "I don't know." I desperately wanted the conversation to move on to something else.

As if granting my wish, a small voice interrupted. "Hey, guys?"

I turned around to see Maya Doshi, her dark eyes wide and anxious. Maya was a new girl in our school this year. Her family moved to town when they opened up an Indian restaurant on Main Street. Maya seemed very nice, but she was so shy it was hard to get to know her. She looked so nervous standing there waiting for one of us to respond.

I smiled to put her at ease. "Hi, Maya. What's up?"

"I'm sorry," her tiny voice said. "I hope I'm not interrupting anything."

"Nope," Darcy said.

"I have to go fix my makeup before class," Fiona said, standing up. "Later, gators."

I gestured for Maya to fill Fiona's now empty chair. "Have a seat."

"Oh. All right. . . ." Maya sat and fiddled with the strap on her book bag. She was always a little bit nervous when she had to talk to someone, but it seemed like something was really eating at her.

"Are you okay?" I asked.

She chewed on her lip for a moment, as if she was trying to decide whether or not to say what she'd come over to say. "I need . . . help."

Darcy said, "Help . . . in, like, a class or something?"

"No." Again Maya's eyes got all jittery. Her voice came out even softer than usual. "I need help from Partners in Crime."

17

After helping Fiona solve *her* mystery a few weeks ago, Darcy and I were eager to keep the detective agency running. But we didn't know how to advertise. We're only seventh graders after all, and it's not a real, licensed detective agency.

Fortunately, Fiona was a marketing maven. She said advertising was no different than starting a rumor — make it cool and it will grow by itself. In text messages, passed notes, and hallway whispers, she knew how to get the word out to the kids and keep the grown-ups in the dark.

Fiona told people that we'd solved a problem for her. Rumors about her case varied from us finding out who stole her designer handbag to reuniting her with a long-lost cousin. When anyone asked us, we simply replied that we don't share anything about our cases. Client confidentiality and all that.

The truth was a lot more complicated. No one else at school knows, and it has to stay that way.

And now I knew why Maya looked super nervous. Something was going on! She had a case! Already my heart started beating faster in excitement. All the bad parts of the day — my math disaster, Hunter and Slade being jerks — faded away.

Darcy seemed as intrigued as I was. "What can we do for you?" she asked.

Maya inched her chair closer to the table and spoke in a hushed tone. "Something very strange happened last Saturday night. My parents were working late at the restaurant, and my older sister was out with her friends. I was stuck home watching my baby brother. He was upstairs in his crib sleeping and I was downstairs watching TV, but then . . ."

"Then what?" I leaned forward, hooked.

"I heard this strange noise on the baby monitor."

"Interference?" Darcy said.

Maya's eyes went to the ceiling like she was trying to remember. "No . . . it was voices. Maybe one, maybe more, I couldn't really tell. Most of the words I couldn't make out, but then I clearly heard someone say, 'Get him,' and then a scream."

A chill went through my body, and Darcy gasped. I realized I'd been gripping my sandwich so hard I'd smooshed it.

"Then what happened?" Darcy asked.

The cafeteria was so loud and Maya's voice was so soft. I wished I could make all the other noise disappear. I leaned even farther forward.

Maya said, "I got scared and ran up to my brother's room. But he was in there alone, still sleeping. I dashed back downstairs and listened to the monitor, but it was quiet the rest of the night."

I shivered as I imagined being alone in a house and hearing a voice that didn't belong. Poor Maya. No wonder she was so shaken up.

"How could a voice be on the monitor if no one but the baby was in the room?" I asked, trying to put things together in my head.

"Baby monitors can sometimes pick up other things," Maya explained. "Other noises or even other conversations if someone else in the area has a monitor, too."

So at least the stranger wasn't *in* her house. But still . . . hearing voices like that. Mega-creepy. Fiona had picked a bad time to leave the table. She'd missed this entire story. I'd have to fill her in later.

I asked, "What would you like us to do?"

Maya looked around nervously. "Maybe help me try to find out who it was. What happened to the person. I told my mom, but she said it was nothing. Probably just someone's television." Maya paused. "It sounded like more than that to me."

Maya seemed like such a caring person, all worried about this stranger in the night. I didn't think it was very realistic that we'd ever find out who it was, though. I hated to disappoint her, but this case was impossible. I said softly, "It was a one-time thing, Maya, so we'd never be able to —"

"No, it wasn't," Maya interrupted. "I haven't told you that part yet. It happened twice. Two Saturdays in a row. The first time I was half asleep on the couch and thought I'd left the TV on. When the voices stopped, I opened my eyes and realized the TV was off. I figured maybe I'd been dreaming, but now that it happened again, I know it was real."

Darcy drummed her fingers on her chin. "Now *this* we can work with. It happened more than once and both times were on a Saturday night?"

"Yes. That's right," Maya said.

"Then that's a pattern," I said, getting excited.

"Which means," Darcy added. "It might happen again."

"Will you help me?" Maya asked. "I'd really like to look into this."

"That depends," Darcy said. "Would your parents

21

mind if you had a few friends over to the house while they were at work?"

Maya brightened. "No, not at all."

"Are they working again this Saturday night?" I asked.

"As always, yes." Maya nodded enthusiastically.

Darcy smiled. "Okay, then. Saturday night it is."

Darcy held out her fist and I held out mine. I motioned with my eyes for Maya to join us. We all bumped fists.

Maya asked, "But . . . what are we doing?"

I grinned. "Planning a sleepover stakeout."

Chapter 3

Saturday could not come fast enough. When I woke up that morning, I was antsy with anticipation. Darcy and I weren't heading to Maya's house until after dinner, though, so I kept myself busy all day to make the time pass faster. I took Hubble, my dog, for an extra-long walk. I did my chores. Helped my mom cook dinner (spaghetti and meatballs — yay!). And then, finally, it was time to go.

Since this was my first time at Maya's and it was an actual sleepover, Mom insisted on driving Darcy and me over so she could meet Maya's parents. I told her we could easily ride our bikes there, but she just said that when I'm a mom someday, I'll understand.

I'd asked Fiona to come along, but she was already going to a big birthday bash one of the popular girls was throwing. She was disappointed, though, since a sleepover stakeout sounded totally exciting. But I guess it's tough juggling ten thousand friends. Fiona's social life was so busy she almost needed an assistant.

Darcy and I sat in the backseat surrounded by our sleeping bags and overnight stuff. Darcy was pulling the zipper on the end of her bag back and forth.

I said, "I invited Fiona to come tonight, but she had plans."

The zipper stopped moving. "Why did you invite Fiona?" Darcy asked.

I shrugged. "Because she's in Partners in Crime now."

"I wouldn't say she's *in* Partners in Crime," Darcy said, a bit of annoyance in her voice. "She just helps out sometimes. She doesn't have to be involved with *every* case."

In the agency . . . helping out . . . what was the difference? I pressed my lips together tightly, feeling kind of frustrated. "I didn't think it would be a big deal."

"It's not." Darcy started playing with the zipper again. "I just . . . I guess I wish you'd asked me first."

I wanted to roll my eyes, but I held back. I swear, sometimes Darcy thinks Partners in Crime is all hers. We created it together. She's not the boss. It's called "Partners" for a reason.

The car pulled into the driveway and Mom gasped. "What a beautiful house."

It had already gotten dark out, but there were little lights staked on either side of the driveway. The house was big and white with red shutters. Planting beds overflowed with pretty flowers my mom could name but I could not.

Darcy and I lugged our gear up the walk, and Mom rang the doorbell. A moment later, Mrs. Doshi opened the door with a welcoming smile. Her black hair was pinned up and she wore a long, flowy skirt that went to her ankles.

"You must be Darcy and Norah. Welcome!" She opened the door wide and we stepped in.

"Hey, guys!" Maya ran up to us, looking pretty excited. At the sight of her giant smile, my irritation from the conversation in the car went away. Maya added in a whisper, "You can take your shoes off and put them to the side there. House rule."

Darcy kicked off her black Converse, and I slipped off my green flats. Meanwhile, Mom and Mrs. Doshi were making small talk.

"My husband is working at the restaurant right now," Mrs. Doshi said. "I'm about to go join him, but Maya's older sister will be here to supervise all evening. She's sixteen and very responsible."

Mom must have approved because, after a little more conversation, she gave me a kiss on the cheek and told us to have fun and call in the morning when we wanted to be picked up.

Mrs. Doshi led us into the kitchen and handed us each tall glasses filled with an orange, thick-looking drink. "Mango lassi?" she offered.

I didn't want to be rude and say no, but I was one of the pickiest eaters on the planet and I'd never heard of this concoction.

Maya whispered into my ear, "It's like a smoothie."

Oh! I liked smoothies. I took a sip and it was really good. "Thank you. It's wonderful," I said.

Darcy had started chugging hers as soon as she got it, so she agreed with a muffled "Mmm-hmm!"

Pleased that her guests were happy, Mrs. Doshi picked up her car keys and jacket. "Anya is upstairs in her room if you need anything. Rishi is already asleep in his crib. Anya will take care of him if he wakes. I want you to just enjoy yourself tonight with your friends, Maya."

She placed a kiss on the top of Maya's head. I think Maya was a little embarrassed, but I thought it was nice. Since Maya had moved here only this year and mostly kept to herself at school, this was probably the first time she'd had friends over to her house.

After the front door closed, we finished up our drinks, put the glasses in the sink, and stood around awkwardly for a moment. I really wanted to go sit by the baby monitor and start investigating. But, even though this was our case, it was Maya's house. I didn't want to be too pushy.

Luckily, Darcy had a way of always putting into words what I didn't have the guts to say. "So where's the monitor?" she said, rubbing her hands together.

Maya raised her eyebrows. "Follow me!" First, she grabbed a bowl of popcorn and a package of cookies from the kitchen counter — I realized she'd prepared a bit for our sleepover, which was sweet. Then she led us into the living room. It had cream-colored couches, tall bookshelves, and a pretty red rug. The TV was on, showing a commercial for these trendy new sneakers that light up.

The three of us settled onto the biggest couch and stared at the baby monitor. It stood on the coffee table, one small blue light shining in its corner. I guess that meant it was on. But what now?

"How do we know when it picks up a sound?" I asked, reaching for some popcorn.

"We'll hear it and this whole area here" — Maya ran her finger over the middle of the monitor — "will light up red."

As soon as she said the words, little red lights trailed across the monitor and then it went dark again. I paused with a kernel of popcorn halfway to my mouth.

"What was that?" Darcy asked, sitting up straight.

Maya frowned. "Nothing. Just movement upstairs. It picks up any little noise."

The lights lit up again and then a pounding came from behind us. I felt a jab of fear.

Maya sighed and sank so far down into the couch, it looked as if she was trying to disappear. "Oh no," she whispered. "I think *Anya's* coming downstairs."

The way Maya said the words, it sounded like her sister was a feared demon, not a junior in high school.

"Has she heard the voice, too?" Darcy asked, looking over her shoulder. The footsteps went into the kitchen. "Maybe we could interview her for the investigation."

"No!" Maya said urgently. "She doesn't know about it. Don't ask her anything."

Sheesh. I knew Maya was shy and all, but this was her sister.

A minute later, the footsteps entered the room along with the sounds of ice clinking against glass. Anya came around the couch and stood in front of us with a drink in her hand. She wore a tank top and little shorts — probably her pajamas — and gave Maya a cold stare.

"So this is why I had to stay in tonight?" she snapped. "So you and your *friends* could sit around and watch TV?"

I didn't like the way she said "friends." As if Maya was paying us to be here or something. As a matter of fact, I didn't like the tone of anything she'd said. No wonder Maya was afraid of her.

"I didn't make you stay in," Maya replied in a small voice.

"No, but Mom did. Because she didn't want you to have to watch Rishi while you had friends over. Meanwhile, Rishi's fast asleep, you guys are just watching lame TV, and I'm missing a party."

She huffed and flipped her hair over her shoulder, then stormed back up the stairs. The monitor flared red with each pounding footstep.

"Well, isn't she a ray of sunshine," Darcy said.

The tightness left Maya's shoulders now that Anya was gone. "She's not always that bad," she said. "She's very nice when my parents are here."

I offered her a sad smile. That must stink to have a mean sister. Like Darcy, I was an only child and had always wondered what it would be like to have a sibling. Now I was kind of glad I didn't.

To change the subject, I suggested we get comfy in our pj's and *actually* watch some TV while keeping our ears pricked up for the monitor. Darcy and Maya agreed, though Darcy still looked angry about Anya's attitude.

I put on my favorite pajama pants — blue with white puffy clouds — and a Danville Middle School sweatshirt. Darcy wore a black T-shirt with the words *Freak of Nature* in white, which perfectly matched her black-and-white skull pajama pants. Maya's pj's were yellow and baggy, making her look even tinier. It was sort of fun to be having a slumber party, even if Darcy and I were technically on a case.

Darcy moved the coffee table off to the side, and we lined up our three sleeping bags so we all had a good view of both the TV and the monitor. Maya dimmed the lights, and we passed around the popcorn and cookies while we watched some silly reality show. A guy walked onto the stage, juggling lit torches. I thought it was an impressive feat, but the judges told him it wasn't "risky" enough. Darcy snorted at this. My eyes went to the monitor. I really wanted to hear something. But, at the same time, I had to accept the fact that the monitor might stay silent all night.

After a while, all the shows started to blur and my eyes got heavy. Darcy and Maya had fallen silent, too. I tried to keep myself awake, but I had a feeling nothing was going to happen. The baby monitor had been quiet for a while now. Except for when Anya had flushed the toilet upstairs a few minutes ago, but after that, nothing but silence . . . in the dark living

room . . . with only the blue light of the television . . .
I was getting . . . very . . . sleepy . . .

"Help! I can't . . ."

I shot straight up like I'd been given an electrical
shock. Darcy did the same, her hair looking even
more disheveled than usual. Maya rose more slowly,
rubbing her eyes.

"Did you hear that?" Darcy asked.

"Yeah," I whispered, and Maya nodded, looking
terrified. There'd been static, so some of the words
were muffled, but I'd heard it.

And then a voice came again through the monitor.
Two unmistakable words that sent chills from my
head to my toes.

"I'm . . . scared."

Chapter 4

All three of us burst into action, climbing out of our sleeping bags and scrambling to our feet. We started running, following Maya's lead, going up the stairs as fast as we could and pounding down the hallway until we came to a stop outside the closed door of her baby brother's room. A little yellow sign with the name *Rishi* hung on the door. Maya reached out and turned the knob. It released with a click, and the door slowly swung inward.

My pulse raced as we stepped into the darkened room. My eyes were slow to adjust and only made out bumps and shadows that could've been furniture or a hunched-over person, for all I knew. Ragged breaths came from all around me, and though logically I knew the three of us were breathing hard from running up the stairs, it made me think of irrational things like monsters hiding in closets.

Maya ran her hand along the wall. "Where's that dimmer switch?" she said anxiously.

Finally, there was a click and the room was lit by a dim orange glow. We were in a cute little nursery with yellow walls and pictures of elephants and tigers. Rishi was sleeping peacefully in his crib. No creepy person hid in the room, begging for help. The closet was open and no monsters lurked within.

It was just us, standing there in the silence, trying to catch our breath.

"What are you doing?" a voice snapped.

Startled, I whipped around. Anya stood by the door frowning, with her hands on her hips.

Maya said, "We heard a sound in Rishi's room, so we came up to check on him."

Not a lie. Well played, Maya.

Anya's eyes narrowed. "I didn't hear anything. And my room's right next to his."

Darcy stepped forward. "But you were sleeping . . . right?" Her voice was suspicious and she had that look in her eye that she gets when she doesn't trust someone.

I examined Anya. Her eyes weren't glassy. She had no pillow marks on her face. No glaring evidence that she'd just woken up. Though she did have a bit of bedhead, but all that proved was that she'd been lying down.

Anya gave us one last glare and backed out of the room. "Just keep it down, *children*."

I loved the way she talked down to us. And by loved I mean hated with every fiber of my being.

Darcy, Maya, and I quietly made our way back downstairs and sat on the couch. The TV was still on, casting its bluish light over the dark living room.

"I think I know what's going on," Darcy said.

Maya's eyes widened. "You do?"

"You think it's Anya," I said, and Darcy nodded.

"My sister?" Maya's face scrunched up in confusion.

"She has the means and the motive," Darcy said. "She could've easily snuck into the room, whispered those words, and snuck back into her room before we got up there. All just to mess with us . . . you . . . whatever."

I usually rolled my eyes at the conspiracies Darcy came up with, but this one seemed spot-on.

"There are two problems with that theory," Maya said. "First, Anya wasn't here the other two nights I heard the voice. I was home alone with my brother."

"Maybe you thought she was out but she really snuck in to trick you?" Darcy suggested.

Maya shook her head. "I doubt that. Plus, there's the other problem. This is the third time I've heard that voice on the monitor. And it's not Anya's voice."

"How can you tell?" Darcy said. "It's fuzzy. There's so much interference, I couldn't even tell if the voice was male or female."

Darcy was clinging to her theory, but I wasn't so sure. Maya had some good points there. Though Anya *could* have disguised her voice.

"Anya's a definite suspect," I said, "but we need to investigate other possibilities. Gather more evidence. Someone really *could* be scared, and need help. It might not be a prank."

Darcy heaved a sigh. "Yeah, you're right."

I had a thought, and turned to Maya. "Has the monitor ever picked up any other interference before?"

Maya nodded. "When we first got the monitor, it picked up the sounds of a TV show from somewhere. My parents thought it was funny."

"And it never happened again?" I asked.

"They changed the channel thingy," Maya said, pointing at the back of the monitor, "and that seemed to fix it."

I picked up the monitor and saw a switch with two options: channel one and channel two. I wanted to play around with it but didn't want to mess things up.

Darcy's face lit up. "The monitor probably couldn't pick up interference from too far away. Let's go outside and check out the neighbors, see if anyone's watching TV."

Maya wrapped her arms around her chest. "Like . . . sneak around in the dark and look in their windows?"

I understood how scary it sounded, but being a detective with Darcy had helped me become a bit braver. "We won't have to get that close," I explained to Maya. "At this time of night, people watch TV with the lights off." I pointed at the TV in front of us as an example. "All we have to do is look for the glow."

We slipped our shoes on and headed outside. The crisp night air was chilly against my cheeks, and I was really glad I'd worn a sweatshirt. We walked down the sidewalk and stopped in front of Maya's neighbor. All the lights in the house were off. "Looks like it's all dark in this one," I whispered.

"They might have a TV room in the back, though," Darcy pointed out. "We should circle the house."

Maya and I murmured in agreement. We tried to walk stealthily along the side of the house, but dead leaves and twigs kept crackling under our shoes. The moon was only a sliver of light in the black sky. Goose bumps rose up on my arms, but not from the cold.

I suddenly had the feeling we were being watched.

My eyes roamed all around . . . left, right. I was casting a nervous glance over my shoulder when I slammed into something.

"Ouch!"

Whoops. I'd walked right into Darcy. "Sorry," I whispered. It would've been helpful if we'd thought to bring a flashlight. Darcy was dressed so dark, and with her black hair, I could barely see her.

She stepped behind and nudged me forward. "You lead the way, blondie."

Great. My hair was being used as a torch. And now we'd reached the back of the house, which edged the woods. And I had to go first. I squinted over at Maya's house, mentally calculating how long it would take to run to the door if something happened.

"Keep going," Darcy whispered from behind me. Maya hadn't made a sound.

I turned the corner into the neighbor's backyard. They only had a small patch of grass before the border of the woods. I shivered involuntarily. Woods at night creeped me out.

"Nothing," Maya said in her small voice. "All dark."

I tore my eyes from the spooky trees and looked at the reason we were standing there to begin with: the neighbor's house. It was all dark from the back, too. No TV light.

Something crunched underneath my shoe. I reached down and picked up a small white piece of paper. It was hard to see with only the light of the moon, but it looked like a drawing of some kind. I stuffed it in my pocket to check it out later.

"Okay," Darcy said, glancing from me to Maya. "One down. We should check the neighbor on the other side of Maya's house and then maybe two or three houses across the street."

My mouth fell open. *We had to do this several more times?!* I didn't think my heart could take it.

But before I could protest, a noise silenced us. A cracking twig. Like the sounds we'd made walking back here.

"What was that?" I asked in a tone that was hushed but also clearly terrified.

Darcy's eyes went wide, and Darcy didn't scare easy. She said, "A person stalking us, a big animal, aliens come to abduct us . . ."

Her imagination was really limitless. Maya let out a little squeak of terror.

I spun around, trying to see anything at all. "Where did the noise come from?"

"I . . . I couldn't tell," Darcy said. "Maybe the woods. Maybe between the houses."

Maya hugged herself. "We should go back inside."

Another crack.

I whipped around and narrowed my eyes at the

woods. I thought my heart was going to burst out of my chest.

Another crack.

"It's not in the woods," Darcy said. "It's behind us. Between the houses."

How were we supposed to get back to Maya's if someone was blocking our way? I reached out and grabbed Darcy's arm. Somehow I felt safer knowing she was right next to me. "What should we do?" I whispered.

The whites of Darcy's eyes flicked back and forth in the darkness. "Two choices. Walk toward Maya's house and find out who or what is over there. Or head into the woods and hide."

I didn't like either of those options.

But soon the choice was taken away from us. The footsteps quickened, got louder and closer. It was too late to hide in the woods. We were frozen to the spot. And a dark shadow emerged from between the houses, the way we'd come.

"Anya?" Maya's trembling voice called out.

"Nope," the voice in the darkness said. A mean-sounding boy's voice.

Chapter 5

The tall, dark figure emerged from the shadows and let out a mocking laugh.

A laugh that I recognized.

"Hunter?" I asked shakily.

He clicked on a flashlight and held it under his chin, illuminating his face. Yep. It was Hunter Fisk, seventh-grade mean kid. My fear morphed into annoyance. But at least he wasn't a man-eating animal or an alien or anything else Darcy had brought up.

I hadn't even realized I'd been digging my fingernails into Darcy's skin until she said, "How about you take your talons out of my arm before I start bleeding?"

"Oh, sorry." I let go and brought my hands down to my sides.

She whispered, "It's okay. I was kind of scared, too." She added with a wink, "But I'll never admit it."

Then she turned to Hunter, and her voice went from soft to hard. "What are you doing out here?"

He took the flashlight from his face and shined it into our eyes. "I should be asking you that. This is *my* house."

I knew that Hunter lived on Maya's street. He'd been teasing her on the way home from school a while back, and Zane had started walking her home to protect her. Which meant that Zane also lived in one of these houses, but I tried to focus on the subject at hand.

"We heard something and we were just checking it out," I said. "We're on our way back in now."

I started to move, but Hunter said, "Wait." He seemed suddenly intrigued. "What did you hear?"

I paused a moment for Maya to explain, but when she didn't, I said, "It was a mysterious voice. Asking for help."

"Male or female?" he asked.

"We couldn't tell," Darcy said. "Too much static."

Hunter moved closer. At least we could all see one another better with his flashlight bouncing around. "One voice or lots of voices?"

"We don't know," Darcy replied again. "There was interference. It was muffled."

Hunter stared at us suspiciously. I silently scoffed. Like we were the untrustworthy troublemakers in this circle? Puh-leeze.

"So you really heard this voice all the way inside Maya's house?" he asked.

We all shared a look. Silently trying to decide whether we should tell him the truth.

Maya gave in. "We heard it over the baby monitor. Sometimes those things can pick up other electronic devices, so we came out to see if any of the neighbors were watching TV."

Hunter furrowed his eyebrows. "Well, I was playing video games, but there was no talking. Just shooting aliens."

Something about that didn't make sense. I crossed my arms and narrowed my eyes at him. "Then what are you doing out here?"

"My TV faces that window." He pointed and we all looked up at the now dark window that faced the backyard and the woods. "I thought I saw something out there in the dark. So I shut the game off and went up real close to the window to see if it would happen again, but then I heard voices. That's when I came out and found you guys creeping around outside."

"So the voices were probably us," Darcy said. "But what did you see before that?"

He looked down and shuffled his feet back and forth, as if he was embarrassed to say it.

"Come on, Hunter," I said. "We told you what we heard. Tell us what you saw."

"It just . . . it doesn't make much sense. It was probably nothing."

"Spill!" Darcy yelled.

He groaned. "Fine. I saw a small light. Moving around outside. It was real quick and just sort of shot by in the dark."

Maybe Darcy's alien theory wasn't too far off.

"But it was nothing," he said quickly. "It was probably from staring at the video game too long. My mom's always on me about that. She's probably right."

"That doesn't explain the voice we heard," Maya said.

Hunter cocked his head to the side as if a thought had just occurred to him. "Could the voice have been an old lady?"

I shrugged. "Anything's possible. Like we said, it wasn't clear."

"I bet I know who it is, then." Hunter put the flash-light under his chin again. His whole face lit up orange and distorted. He made his voice go deep and creepy as he said each word slowly, "It . . . was . . . the . . . Old Witch."

I took in a sharp breath. "Who?"

Maya gasped, "What?"

"You don't know about her? You should. She lives right across the street from you," Hunter told Maya smugly. "Someone in the neighborhood should have warned you when you moved in."

"A person lives in that run-down old house?" Maya asked, surprised. "I've never seen anyone."

"She hardly ever comes out," Hunter said, adding a dash of menace to his voice. "Only once every few years, when it's time for her to lure an innocent child into her house . . . for sacrifice."

Darcy groaned. "You're full of it, Hunter."

"No, he's kind of right," another voice said.

Startled, I jumped and turned around. A shadow was walking toward us, from the house next to

Hunter's, two doors down from Maya. Hunter shined the flashlight at the figure, and my throat went dry.

Zane Munro.

I slowly blinked a few times as he joined our group.

Zane was here. Standing right next to me. And I was wearing cloud pants. I closed my eyes and prayed for Darcy's aliens to beam me up. I opened my eyes again. No luck. Still here in my dorky pajamas.

"What do you mean 'kind of right'?" Darcy asked.

Zane stuffed his hands in the pockets of his athletic pants. "There is a woman who lives across the street and hardly ever comes out. And she is very strange. But I don't believe those stories about her."

Hunter said, "Well, then how did she get the name the Old Witch?"

Zane shrugged. "Probably from kids referring to her as 'that old witch.' You know how these stories get started."

Hunter shook his head. "It's more than that. She lives alone in that giant house and she's, like, a thousand years old. No one in the neighborhood can remember her ever being young."

My logical brain told me that Hunter was only

trying to scare us, but my illogical heart pounded wildly. Between hearing the voice on the monitor, sneaking around in the dark, and listening to a story about a witch, this was turning into one creepy night.

"Maya!" a shrill voice shrieked.

We all jumped, even the boys. Footsteps pounded the dead leaves on the ground as Anya stomped over to us. Arms crossed over her chest, she yelled, "What are you *children* doing out here?"

Again with the emphasis on "children." Sigh.

Maya shrank back. If she was a turtle, she would have just retreated into her shell. "We're hanging out, Anya," she said. "I didn't think we had to stay in the house. You're in charge of Rishi tonight."

"Well, I'm in charge of you three, too." She pointed at Maya, Darcy, and me. "And I came downstairs to find you gone. What if something had happened to you when I was in charge? Mom and Dad would kill me."

No, don't worry about the mysterious, awful thing that happened to us in that scenario, Anya. The more important thing is that you would've been punished. I made a mental note to thank my parents for keeping me an only child.

"Get in the house!" Anya ordered, then stormed back the way she came.

The three of us turned to follow her. The fun was over, for now.

I glanced over my shoulder to wave good-bye to Zane, but he looked uncharacteristically serious.

"Find me at school on Monday," he said, eyes set intently on me. "I have to tell you something."

Chapter
6

I loved science class. And this term we were studying weather, which — though it wasn't astronomy — was still pretty cool. But Mr. Mahoney was tough. He's the Simon Cowell of teachers. You could get every question right and he'd point out that your handwriting could've been better. But, even so, I wasn't expecting the horror that landed on my desk Monday.

We'd had a quiz the previous week on converting Celsius to Fahrenheit and vice versa. There were only four problems and I'd thought it was pretty easy. As Mr. Mahoney passed the graded quizzes back, I sat at my desk, thinking excitedly about Zane wanting to tell me something, and remembering the crazy night at Maya's house.

Darcy, who sat in front of me, got her quiz back first, and I saw a 100 scrawled at the top of hers. When I got mine, though, there was a giant 75 in bold at the top. There was also a note from Mr. Mahoney that said: *See me.*

My stomach dropped into my feet. Possibly onto the floor. It probably rolled down the hall and into the bathroom to throw up on its own.

What could've gone wrong? I wondered. To convert Celsius to Fahrenheit, you multiply the temperature by nine, divide that answer by five, and then add thirty-two. I checked out the problem with a big red X next to it. *Convert 38 degrees Celsius to Fahrenheit.* Okay . . . 38 times 9 is 342; 342 divided by 5 is 68.4. And that plus 32 is 100.4. And that was the answer I had written down. What the heck? Had Mr. Mahoney made a mistake?

I had trouble paying attention during the rest of the class. I couldn't wait for it to be over so I could show Mr. Mahoney that I'd gotten the problem right. Finally the bell rang. I picked up my stuff, told Darcy I'd meet her in the next class, and walked up to Mr. Mahoney's desk.

He looked at me from under his big bushy eyebrows. "Norah Burridge, what can I do for you?"

I held the paper out. "You wrote 'see me' on my quiz and you marked an answer wrong that wasn't really wrong."

"Ah, yes," he said in his gravelly voice. "Well, Norah, your calculations were correct, but the answer was certainly wrong."

Huh?

Mr. Mahoney stood and walked over to the far left side of the board, where the four quiz questions still remained. "You correctly calculated that 38 degrees Celsius is 100.4 degrees Fahrenheit. However, what was the question?"

I stepped closer to the board. *Oh no.* Question number four wasn't "convert 38 degrees," it was "convert 30 degrees." I'd copied the wrong number down from the board. Just like I had done with my math homework last week. What was wrong with me? Was I having trouble focusing? Maybe running Partners in Crime on top of my homework was too much?

"This note is for your parents." He handed me a folded-up piece of paper. "I've noticed you squinting a lot in class, especially when you try to read the board. And now this mistake as well. I'm recommending that you get your eyes checked." At my blank look, he added, "You may need glasses."

I didn't know if that was bad news or good news. It *would* explain why I'd been having those mess-ups lately. But . . . glasses?! I couldn't imagine them on me.

My shoulders sagged. I took the note and turned to leave. "Thank you, Mr. Mahoney."

"Norah," he said. His voice was a little softer than the one he used in class. "If you do need glasses, let me know and I'll change your grade."

But even that didn't make me feel better.

Darcy passed me a note in English.

> Partners in Crime meeting. After school. You, me, Fiona. The Java Lamp. We need to come up with our next steps for Maya's case.

I smiled, pleased that she'd gotten over whatever was bothering her the other day and had invited Fiona along. I scribbled back: *I'm in.* Then I pretended to yawn, stretching my arms up into the air so I could drop the note onto Darcy's desk behind me.

The prospect of getting one of those giant face-size cookies from the Java Lamp made me feel a little bit better after my "I may need glasses" revelation. What was also making me feel better was knowing that I had an excuse to talk to Zane sometime today. But about what?

I was reminded of a conversation I'd had with Maya when Darcy and I were working on our first case. Maya had been nervous to talk to me, as usual, but then she'd blurted out that Zane had a secret.

She never told me what it was, which really stank. But at the same time, it made me like Maya more because she could obviously be trusted with secrets. After Hunter started teasing Maya on the way home from school, Zane had walked with her to protect her. And they'd become friends. I'd wondered if the big secret was that they were becoming boyfriend and girlfriend, but it didn't seem like that was it.

After the last bell, I hung around my locker, wondering if Zane might stop by. I didn't want to be standing there doing nothing and looking desperate. So I reached into my book bag front pocket, where I'd stashed the piece of paper I'd found on the ground behind Hunter's house Saturday night.

I squinted, trying to make sense of what I was seeing. It looked like some sort of swirly design. Was it three connected butterflies? No, the thing on the right looked like a butterfly, or a sideways heart, but the rest of it . . . I shrugged and stuffed it back into my backpack. It was just someone's elaborate doodle. Not a clue.

I wondered if Zane was waiting for me at *his* locker, so I closed mine and walked down the opposite hallway to find him. I didn't know which locker number was his but knew it was in this block. I stopped, looked around, and sighed. He wasn't there. I stood still for a moment, trying to decide whether I should give up and leave. Then a big hand grabbed my upper arm and spun me around.

"Hey, Norah," Slade said in a mocking tone. "I hear the Old Witch is after you."

Great. Hunter had told his best friend about Saturday night. Just what I needed. More taunting from Slade.

He did his best evil witch cackle, throwing his head back and laughing. His fingers were still wrapped around my arm. I tried to pull away, but his grip only tightened.

Darcy came up beside me and growled, "Take your hand off my best friend or I will punch you into next week."

Wow. A time-traveling beatdown. Darcy's threats were creative.

Slade let go, but his dark eyes never left mine. "Watch out." He pointed at us as he stepped backward. "One of you girls is next. The witch is hungry."

"Ignore him," Darcy said, leading me away. "Someone's waiting for you at your locker."

Chapter 7

Apparently, Zane had been waiting for me while I was waiting for him. We must have passed in the hallway, but since I was apparently half blind, I hadn't noticed. Now, though, as I rounded the corner, I saw him leaning against my locker. And, I swear, when he saw me, his eyes lit up.

My heart did a little flutter thing, but I told myself to be brave.

"So," I said when I reached the locker, "what's your secret?"

Zane's eyes widened. His mouth dropped open and he didn't say anything at first. Then, "Secret? What do you mean?"

"Saturday night . . . you said you had to tell me something."

"Oh, right." His expression returned to normal, relieved even. "It's not a secret, though. Just something you guys need to know."

You guys. Meaning me, Darcy, maybe Maya. He wasn't spilling whatever secret he had right now. Though, from the look on his face, he definitely had one.

"What do we need to know?" Darcy asked.

"When we were walking home from school last Friday," Zane began, "Maya told me you guys had opened a case to help her figure out that weird voice she'd heard. She told me you were coming over for a sleepover Saturday night and she was soooo excited. She was actually talking loud for once. Maybe . . . too loud."

Darcy scratched at her dark mop of hair. "Go on. . . ."

"Hunter was walking behind us," Zane said. "I can't be sure if he heard or not, but —"

"There's a chance he knew we were having the sleepover," I said, filling in the rest. "And he might have done the voice thing, to freak us out."

"So he didn't come outside because he heard us walking through his yard," Darcy chimed in. "He knew about everything ahead of time. He'd set it up."

"Maybe," I said, not wanting to get ahead of ourselves. "There's also a chance he *didn't* hear your conversation, right?"

Zane nodded. "I can't be sure either way. I just thought you should know."

"Thanks." I smiled.

Darcy's phone buzzed and she checked it. "Fiona just texted. She's at the café already and has three cookies with our names on them."

As much as I wanted to stay and chat with Zane longer, you can't keep Darcy from waiting cookies. So I was whisked away with barely enough time to wave good-bye.

"I don't know if this is possible, but it tastes even better this time," Darcy said through a mouthful of cookie.

The Java Lamp was busy. Conversation and laughter filled the air while music played lightly from the speakers in the ceiling.

I nibbled at my cookie. Darcy was right — it was fantastic. I took small bites to make it last longer. Even though, compared to other cookies, this one was Jupiter-size. (That's the largest planet in our solar system. Just so you know.)

"Thank you, Abigail Mattimore," Darcy said, and we all laughed. If Abigail hadn't gone all psycho over where Trey went on Fridays, we wouldn't have been on the case that led us here.

We all held our cookies up and toasted. "To Abigail!"

We filled Fiona in on everything that had happened on Saturday night, including Slade's threat about the Old Witch, and Zane's warning about Hunter.

"So now we're thinking it might all be some sort of prank," Darcy finished up.

"Did anyone talk to Maya today?" Fiona asked.

"I didn't," I said, feeling a little bit guilty about it. But, in my defense, I had a lot on my mind. A bad grade on my science quiz, the possibility of wearing glasses the rest of my life, and Zane, for starters. Still, I should have stopped and said hi to Maya at some point, even if we didn't have anything new on the case.

Darcy chugged from her glass, leaving a chocolate milk mustache above her lip. "I didn't either. But, to be honest, I barely notice the girl. She's so small and quiet."

I frowned, imagining what it must be like moving to town in the seventh grade when all the other kids know one another. Add Maya's natural shyness on top of it . . .

"We should try harder to talk to her during the day," I said. "She's only lived here a few weeks and has no friends."

Darcy said, "But she's a client."

"So?" I crossed my arms. "Fiona was a client and now she's our friend. Aren't you glad we talked to her?"

"She *did* buy me this cookie," Darcy said with a smirk. Fiona jokingly stuck her tongue out at her.

"Moving on," I said. "Let's make a list of suspects."

Darcy whipped her case notebook out of her backpack. It was just a regular notebook with a black cover, but we used it only for Partners in Crime business.

"Let's start with the obvious," I said. "Hunter Fisk."

"Evidence?" Darcy said, pencil poised to fill in the column.

I listed off, "He lives right next door to Maya. He may have heard that we were coming over. And he just *happened* to come outside to scare us when we were investigating. Plus, he has a history of teasing Maya."

Darcy finished writing and moved on to the next column. "Motive?"

I thought for a moment. "Does being a jerk in general count?"

Darcy nodded. "I'll write 'bully behavior.' "

Fiona had been twirling a strand of hair around her finger while we talked. Now she stopped and said, "Wait a second. Hunter heard about the sleepover the day before."

"Yeah, so," Darcy said.

"But Maya first heard the voice long before that," Fiona said.

Duh! I'd always underestimated Fiona's smarts. "That's true," I said to Darcy. "She heard it on two Saturdays before Hunter knew about our sleepover. So maybe Hunter came out to scare us the night of the sleepover, but he has nothing to do with the voice."

Darcy frowned at this complication. "Next suspect."

"What about the Old Witch?" Fiona asked.

"That's just a story," I said. "She doesn't abduct kids or any of that stuff."

"Yeah, but the voice still could've been her, right?" Fiona said.

Good point. I nodded and Darcy spoke as she wrote. "Evidence: lives across the street, is creepy. Motive: to eat children."

I rolled my eyes. "Oh, please."

Darcy snickered. "It's in pencil. I can always change it."

"Okay, next suspect," I said, wanting to move this thing along.

Darcy tapped the pencil on the table. "Zane Munro."

I gasped. "What?"

Darcy shrugged. "We have as much evidence on him as we do the others. He lives a couple houses down from Maya. *And* he was outside the night of the sleepover."

I stammered, "But — but he would never! What motive could he possibly have?"

Darcy held her hands up. "I have 'to eat children' down as one motive here. Obviously, it's too early in the case for motives. We can't exclude any suspects from the list just because you have a huge crush on them."

My face turned a fiery red. If I were a volcano, hot steaming magma would have been shooting out of my head.

"Girls, girls," Fiona said. "Let's focus on facts here. Right now, any neighbors of Maya's are suspects."

"And really," I said, "*suspect* is too harsh a word. The person didn't do anything wrong."

"Creeping Maya out is wrong," Darcy said.

"But we still don't know for sure that someone's trying to scare Maya," I protested. "Isn't it more likely that something is really going on outside on Saturday nights, and whoever is involved has no idea that Maya can hear them on the baby monitor?"

Fiona leaned back in her chair. "How could a baby monitor just pick up a conversation from outside the house? I think we need to know more about how those baby monitor thingies work."

Darcy reached into her backpack and whipped out a bunch of papers she had printed out from various websites. "Done!"

I looked through the stack. There was a lot of tech jargon and articles about frequency interference. Darcy had really done her research. Unfortunately, she'd have to translate.

The song playing through the café speakers ended and I waited for a few seconds until the next song started. We didn't need to whisper when the music covered our conversation.

"What does all this mean?" I asked.

Darcy folded her hands on top of the table. "Imagine that the baby monitor is like a tiny radio station. And the little plastic antenna is the radio station's transmitter. Anyone within range of the radio station can pick up whatever music is playing, as long as they have a radio."

Following along, I said, "So anyone who has the same baby monitor can hear whatever is said?"

"It doesn't even have to be the same one. Or even a baby monitor. It just has to use the same frequency and be within the range."

"What do you mean, frequency?" Fiona asked.

"It's like a bandwidth . . . or a channel. So as long as someone is transmitting on that channel, whether it's from another baby monitor, a CB radio, a walkie-talkie, or whatever, if they're in range, then you can possibly hear it on your monitor."

65

I flipped to the next page in Darcy's stack and saw an article about problems with baby monitors in close quarters. "What's this all about?"

Darcy looked at the article. "Oh, it's about the challenges people face when there are several families living in the same apartment building. If they have the most common types of baby monitors, they can hear all sorts of stuff from each other's apartments. So they have to be sure to buy a more expensive monitor or one that doesn't work on the same frequency as their neighbors."

"What kind does Maya's family have?" Fiona said.

Darcy grinned. "Interesting that you ask." She pulled the bottom paper from the stack. "Theirs is the Baby Sounds 2000. The most inexpensive model, at only sixteen dollars. And therefore one of the most common."

"So maybe all we have to do is figure out if any of her neighbors have the same one," I said.

"How do we do that?" Fiona said.

"We can start by seeing if anyone even has a baby," Darcy said. "Maya probably wouldn't know, though, since she just moved in."

Hmm. That was true. And she was shy enough talking to her peers. Talking to strangers must be even worse. "We could find a way to ask around," I suggested. "But first we need to know what the range is, right?" I aimed my question at Darcy since she was the pro at tech stuff.

Darcy drummed her black-painted fingernails on the tabletop and smiled. "Leave that to me."

Chapter

8

I slid into my seat in social studies a few minutes before the bell. The required reading pages for that night were written on the board, so I pulled out my notebook to copy them down. I reminded myself to double- and triple-check afterward that I'd written the right numbers.

Darcy sat next to me and peered at my notebook. "What are you doing, testing your signature?" She added in a dreamy, singsong voice, "Ms. Munro. Mrs. Norah Munro. Mrs. Norah Burridge-Munro."

I resisted the urge to cover her mouth with my hand. "I'm copying the assignment off the board, Darcy," I hissed. "You should be doing the same thing."

Darcy chuckled. But then she stopped. "Why are you making that face? You're not really mad, are you? You know I'm just kidding around."

Totally confused, I said, "What face?"

"That squinty-eyed look you were just giving the board. Like you wanted to kill it."

I groaned. In all the case drama, I hadn't had a chance to tell my BFF about my news. "I'm squinting because I can't read the board very well. I might . . . need glasses."

"Oh," Darcy said slowly, making a giant O with her mouth. "When did you find out? Why didn't you tell me sooner?"

I felt a pang of guilt. It was true; Darcy and I usually told each other everything immediately. "Just yesterday," I explained. "I'm going to the eye place tonight." After reading the note from Mr. Mahoney, Mom and Dad had spared no time in getting me a quick appointment at an eyeglass place at the mall. They also conveniently make your glasses in one hour as you wait, so tomorrow I could be showing up at school with four eyes.

Darcy shook her head. "And I'm getting my stupid braces on this afternoon!"

I patted her hand. "That stinks. I'm sorry," I said sadly.

"But hey," Darcy said, brightening, "I did some Internet research last night on the range of Maya's baby monitor. I have computer lab next. If I finish the class work early, I'm going to use the rest of the time to figure out the area of Maya's neighborhood we have to work with."

"Cool," I said. I had no doubt she'd finish her computer work early.

Mrs. Feldman, our social studies teacher, strolled in and started talking about a new project we had to work on: a paper on World War II. She said, "You can work on this project individually or in teams of two."

Darcy looked over at me and whispered, "Partners?"

"Always," I said back with a smile.

AFTER the last bell, Fiona came up to my locker and said, "Close your eyes and say 'oh' real slow."

Um, ooookay. Though I was suspicious, I let my eyes close and said, "Ohhhhhh," until I felt a gooey grossness on my lips. My eyes snapped open and caught Fiona with a little pink wand in her hand. It was a lip gloss sneak attack.

"What are you doing?" I snapped.

Fiona shook her head and capped the gloss. "It was wrong."

"Yeah, no kidding. You can't just walk up to some unsuspecting person and makeup them."

She rolled her eyes and put one hand on the hip of her belted red sweaterdress. "I'm not saying I *did* anything wrong. I'm saying my *idea* was wrong. I thought the thing your look was missing was a little shimmering lip color. But that's not it."

I almost growled at her. "Fiona. Just give up already. I look how I look."

She tilted her head to the side. "When astrologers find some new thing in the sky and they don't know what it is, do they give up?"

"It's astronomers, actually, but no, they don't."

"Then I'm not giving up either. I will find the right stylistic choice for you. If it's the last thing I do!" She raised her fist in the air dramatically.

Darcy chose that moment to walk up to my locker. She raised her eyebrows. "I don't know if I should ask what's going on or run like the wind."

"Run," I said, laughing. "Run while you can."

She waved a piece of paper in the air. "But then I wouldn't be able to show you guys where our suspects live. . . ."

I snatched the paper out of her hand. "You did it? You figured out the range? You're a genius!"

Darcy gave a little bow.

Fiona peeked over my shoulder. "What are we looking at here?"

I squinted at the paper. Now that I realized I was doing it so much, it seemed like I was squinting all the time. I brought it closer to my face, and the photo got clearer. It was a satellite picture, an aerial view. "This is Maya's neighborhood," I said.

"Once I found out the range of the baby monitor," Darcy explained, "I figured out the radius around Maya's house that her monitor could pick up. Then I used Google Earth and Maps to create this."

"Go, you!" Fiona said to Darcy, sounding impressed. I was impressed as well, but I'd expect nothing less from my tech-savvy BFF.

Darcy pointed at the house in the center. "That's Maya's." Her finger moved down and to the left. "This is Hunter's."

And the one to the left of that was Zane's, I thought to myself.

A red circle was drawn over the map, with Maya's house in the middle. Inside the circle were two houses across the street, a large chunk of the woods behind Maya's house, one big house to the right, Hunter's house on the left, and half of Zane's house.

"So," I said, "if we stood in any area inside the circle and used some equipment that transmitted on that frequency, Maya could hear it on her monitor?"

"As long as her monitor was on at the time, yeah," Darcy said.

This was really good work. My heart pumped with anticipation. "Now we know exactly where it could be coming from," I said. "Great job narrowing it down!"

Darcy beamed. "Thanks! And now we can case the neighborhood after school tomorrow and figure out if anyone in those houses has a baby."

"Tomorrow?" I said. "Let's do it now!" I was really excited. This was our first solid lead.

"Yeah, I can't do it tomorrow," Fiona said.

"But I can't do it now." Darcy looked at me. "I'm getting my braces, remember?"

Oh yeah. But I didn't want to wait until tomorrow to get answers we could have now. "Fiona and I will do it today," I said brightly. "And then we'll text you or call with what we find out."

Darcy's expression soured. "But . . . what will you say to people when they come to the door? I'm the best liar in our agency," she added modestly.

That was true. I was about to backtrack when Fiona said, "Leave it to me. I was the lead in the school play last year. Acting is just like lying, right?"

"Right," Darcy said coolly. She put the piece of paper into my hand, turned on her heel, and left.

Fiona grimaced. "Wow, she's in a really bad mood because of those braces, huh?"

I nodded slowly but wasn't quite sure. I knew the idea of braces was bothering Darcy. But I had the feeling there was something more going on.

A half hour later, Fiona and I parked our bikes in front of Maya's house. We had Darcy's map, and we had a plan. I knew our story, and Fiona said she'd do most of the talking. So now we just had to start knocking on doors. Meanwhile my nerves were knocking all around my stomach.

I'd been super excited at the prospect of getting answers, but now . . . not so much about walking up and talking to random strangers. Thankfully, Fiona had enough confidence for the both of us.

"Let's see," she said, taking the map. "Half of the circled area is in the woods, so we can skip that, obviously. I know Hunter doesn't have any younger siblings, and his older brother's in college, so no baby monitors there. What about Zane?"

She raised her eyebrows at me. Like I was the authority on Zane Munro. I blushed. "He has a sister, but she's in high school," I said sheepishly. "No babies."

The corner of Fiona's mouth lifted up a bit. "We could knock on his door anyway, just to be sure. . . ."

I gave her a look. "I get this enough from Darcy."

Fiona waved the map at me. "I'm only teasing. I think your crush on him is adorable."

I grimaced. "Wonderful. Glad I could entertain you. Moving on . . ."

Fiona returned her attention to the map. "I

guess we should do the house on the other side of Maya's, then. After that, we'll do the ones across the street."

Anything that got the topic of conversation off The Crush That Would Never Be Returned.

We walked down the sidewalk, skipping over cracks. I always avoided stepping on them, and it was funny to find that Fiona had the same habit. We reached the house on the other side of Maya's and stopped. It was green with dark red shutters. There were no telltale signs of kids — no swing set, basketball hoop, or abandoned tricycle. But there was one car in the driveway, so someone was home.

The owner apparently loved garden gnomes, because they lined the narrow path to the front door. There was a laughing gnome, a napping gnome, a golfing gnome, a guitar-playing gnome, and more. Except one spot where it looked like a gnome had been taken away, and only a small circle of dead grass remained. Maybe he went for gnome repair?

We got to the front door, and Fiona rang the bell. I stood beside her. My hands were fidgeting so much, I put them behind my back.

"Do you remember your lines?" I asked.

Fiona said, "No problem. It's just like a play."

A moment later the front door swung inward and a face appeared behind the screen. He was bald, maybe in his late sixties, and he narrowed his eyes at us.

Oh no. A grumpy old man.

"What're you sellin'?" he snapped.

Fiona smiled wide. "We're not selling anything, sir. As part of a community service project, we're going door to door handing out coupons for diapers to any family with babies or toddlers."

(And hoping that you didn't actually ask for those coupons . . . since we had none.)

We figured if someone really wanted the coupons, Fiona could turn to me, and I could pretend that I thought she'd brought them and we'd wander off pretend-confused.

Hey, we made it up on the way there. It was the best we could do.

The man's frown softened a bit as Fiona continued to flash her giant smile.

"My babies are thirty years old," he said. "But that's a nice thing you're doing."

"Thank you, sir," Fiona said.

And then we backed away. Quickly, before he got grumpy again.

In the house across the street, we found a young woman who only had a million cats. No babies. That left us with only one more house to check.

The Old Witch's house.

Fiona and I stood before it, gazing. The house must have been beautiful years ago, but now it was kind of sad-looking. The pale blue paint was peeling. One of the wooden porch steps sagged. The yard was full of weeds that were probably taller than Maya. The black mailbox was a bit crooked on its post and the stenciled name, WOLFSON, was faded.

"Do we really need to knock on this door?" Fiona's voice trembled a bit. That confidence she'd had before seemed to disappear. "I mean, everyone knows she lives alone."

"If anyone really lives there at all," I whispered. I still wasn't convinced the old lady actually existed.

"Maybe we could just creep up and peek in the windows." As Fiona pointed at the house, the silver bracelets on her wrist jangled.

"You're not exactly dressed for sneaking around," I said, motioning at her loud jewelry. "Let's just go up to the front door and knock like normal people."

"But she definitely doesn't have a baby," Fiona insisted.

"Yeah, but the voice could still be her. Maybe she has a monitor for some other reason. Maybe she needs help right now! At the very least, we can get some clues."

Fiona frowned. "Or get eaten."

I shivered, but we slowly stepped forward, closer to the house. A tiny sound escaped Fiona's lips. Then another. Was she . . . holding back a giggle fit?

"What are you doing?" I asked.

She covered her mouth for a moment, then said, "Sorry. Sometimes I laugh when I get nervous. I can't help it. It happens during horror movies."

"Well, this isn't a horror movie."

"Tell that to the creepiest house in the world!" She pointed at the front door. "I mean, if that's not haunted, I don't know what is."

"Let's just get this over with," I said.

My heart started pounding faster, but my brain told me to move forward. *Use logic*, it said. *She's not a kid-snatching witch. She's just a little old lady.* I gingerly stepped up the rickety porch steps and to the front door. I looked to my side, but Fiona wasn't there. I turned around.

She was still standing down on the grass.

"Fiona!" I hissed. "Get up here! You have to do your lines."

She shook her head. "You do this one. I'll stay here."

I groaned. It seemed I had no choice. My hands were shaking, but I lifted one in the air to make a fist, ready to knock on the door.

Before I could, though, I saw something out of the corner of my eye. The window to my left had a white lace curtain. And it moved, like someone had taken a peek at me.

"Norah?" Fiona said nervously. "Norah, let's go."

No, I thought. I'd come this far. I lifted my fist and knocked three times.

Only silence. I looked at the window again, but the curtain didn't move. I heard a scrape, like someone reaching across the door, maybe to open it. I took one step back.

"Norah! Come on!" Fiona yelled, more insistent now.

A thump came, then a dragging sound, then another thump . . . clump . . . clump . . . coming to a stop right behind the door.

I stepped forward and leaned my face near the wood. "Hello?" I called.

And a voice whispered back, "Go . . . away."

Chapter

9

When you're standing at the front door of the creepiest house you've ever seen and a mysterious voice tells you to go away, you should probably go away. But, though my brain was working, my legs were useless and suddenly felt as if they were made of jelly. I was frozen. And therefore couldn't run.

Fear squeezed my heart like a stress ball. I looked over my shoulder for help from Fiona, but she had already run across the street and was standing safely in Maya's front yard. She held her hands up in the air. A gesture that clearly meant *What are you doing? Get over here!*

I forced myself to take a deep, calming breath. I tried to reason with my panicked muscles. *An old witch does not live in this house. Those stories are made up. If she wanted to abduct me and cook me in her hearth, she already had plenty of time to do it since I've been standing here like a dummy.*

The wood beneath my feet creaked. The woman was still standing there on the other side of the door. I coughed feebly.

The voice came again, "What do you want?"

Startled, my eyes opened wider. Something was different about the voice, though. Instead of trying to scare *me*, the woman sounded fearful herself. I struggled to remember the name I'd seen on the battered mailbox. I nervously licked my lips and said, "Um, Mrs. Wolfson?"

Suddenly a bunch of sounds came from within. She must've unlocked three or four dead bolts. Then the door swung inward.

For a supposed witch who abducted and ate children, she didn't look very intimidating. Her long hair was held up in a bun, and wisps of gray framed her thin face. She wore a long housedress and held a cane. That must have been what had caused the clunking sound.

She eyed me warily. "Yes?"

I glanced frantically over my shoulder at Fiona, who was now hiding behind a hedge, probably watching the action and shaking. All that was visible of her were her high-heeled booties — totally inappropriate detective gear, by the way. I turned back to Mrs. Wolfson and racked my brain for something to say. I decided to go with something close to the truth. "I'm sorry to bother you. Um, my friend lives across the street and she heard some strange noises and I just wanted to check to make sure you were all right."

Mrs. Wolfson's hard eyes softened. "Oh. I'm fine, dear. Thank you for checking."

"Okay." My legs decided they could work again, so I began to back away. "Have a nice day."

She held out a pale, bony hand. "Wait . . ."

I swallowed and my throat felt tight. "What is it?" *Please don't let this be the part where she turns evil and abducts me.*

"I'm sorry I was rude to you before. I thought it was those dang Danville boys again."

"Who?" I asked.

She waved her hand dismissively. "Just some darn teenagers that come up and knock on my door only because their friends dared them to bother the Old Witch."

I gasped. Mrs. Wolfson let out a loud laugh, and it sounded nothing like a witch's cackle. "You think I don't know about my nickname?" She shrugged. "I don't mind it too much. People leave me alone and don't try to sell me stuff."

"Oh . . . okay," I said, mainly because I didn't know what else to say.

Her face turned sad, and she began speaking as if she'd been waiting to tell her story. "I know I should have moved after my husband died so long ago. This big old house is too much for me to take care of. I let the lawn go dead and weedy. The paint chipped. And then I was so embarrassed by the house, I stopped socializing with neighbors. I watched out my window as old friends moved away and new people moved in. And I just . . . stayed inside. So I can understand how you kids came up with the nickname and all the rumors. But I don't mean anyone any harm. I just wanted to stay in the house my husband and I bought together. It makes me feel closer to him."

My heart broke into a thousand pieces. "Of course," I said, feeling choked up.

Her voice cracked. "Will you tell the other children I'm not mean? I turn on the outside light on Halloween, but all the children skip my house."

I swallowed hard. "I will personally make sure that doesn't happen this year," I said. And I would keep my promise. Somehow.

I ran across the street to Fiona, who breathlessly asked me for every single detail. I explained that Mrs. Wolfson was not a witch. Just a nice, misunderstood old lady.

I took one last glance at the old run-down house. I had to figure out a way to change the neighborhood's perception of Mrs. Wolfson.

But first, we had to solve Maya's mystery.

And, at the moment, unfortunately, I had to head to the eye doctor.

"Cover your right eye with this and read the top three lines to me."

I took the black plastic thingamabob from the eye doctor. It looked like a ladle, but I used it to cover my eye like he said and then squinted at the chart on the wall.

"E," I said. You'd have to be completely blind not to see the top letter. "F and P for the second line. And then T, O, Z."

"Great." The doctor nodded. He wore glasses and I briefly wondered if he tested himself like this or if he had another doctor do it.

He asked me to keep going. By the time I got to the fifth line, I was squinting.

"O, B, C, L, T . . ." I could make out most of the letters, except the one at the far right. Was that an E or an F? I squinted harder but that didn't help, so I just guessed. "E?"

I looked at the doctor to try to see his reaction, but his face was unreadable. My stomach turned over with anxiety. I reminded myself that getting something wrong here wasn't like failing a test. It wasn't my fault my eyes weren't perfect.

"Okay, now the next line," he said.

This one was much harder. It was so blurry. I blinked a few times, but that didn't help. I read the letters, basically guessing at half of them. "T, E, P, O, L, F, D, Z."

"Hmm, okay. Can you read any letters on the bottom row?"

I squinted, blinked, opened my eye wider, everything I could think of. Then I sighed. "No, not a one."

We repeated the process with my left eye covered. Then I sat my chin on this weird metal contraption and said "better," "worse," or "the same" to a million different combinations of glass the doctor flipped in front of my eyes. After that, he scribbled my prescription on a pad of paper and told Mom and me to head to the showroom to look at frames.

Frames! That meant it was real. . . . I *was* getting glasses. I walked from the dimly lit office into the bright front store area with my shoulders hunched. I'd had a glimmer of hope that this was all some mistake. That the doctor would say, "Your vision is perfect! That teacher didn't know what he was talking about!"

But that didn't happen.

"They have such a great selection here," Mom said, gazing at all the frames. "You'll find a beautiful pair. So many of these would look pretty on you."

There were, like, a hundred frames on display and I think I tried on every one. Red, black, tortoiseshell, wire, plastic, huge, small, narrow, wide, circular, rect-angular. Forced enthusiasm continued to pour from Mom as I picked up each pair. I appreciated that she was trying to make me feel better, but as she oohed and ahhed over all of them, it just didn't help. They all looked the same to me — unnatural. As if it wasn't my face anymore.

I turned to Mom and said hopefully, "How about contact lenses?"

She gave me a half smile, but I knew the answer before she even started talking. "Maybe in high school. Your father and I would like you to wait a couple years."

Part of me wanted to throw myself on the floor like a two-year-old and have a tantrum, but that wouldn't solve my problem. I wouldn't be cured. I'd keep squinting. My grades might drop because of all these mistakes I kept making. I had to face it.

I picked up the tortoiseshell pair. "These ones, I guess."

Mom nodded her approval. "Lovely."

Luckily (or UNluckily), they had my prescription in stock, so I was able to get the lenses fitted into the frames while we waited at the store. The saleslady fit the new glasses onto my nose, and that was that. I sighed.

"Why don't you go wait in the mall while I finish paying?" Mom suggested. She gave me a nudge with her elbow and added, "Maybe the boys will look cuter now that you can see them."

I turned around so she wouldn't see me roll my eyes. I knew she was only trying to put me in a good mood, but come on!

I slunk out into the mall and looked at my reflection in the storefront's glass window. I turned to the side, then faced front again. I guess the glasses didn't look *that* bad. Maybe I was just slow to accept change. They'd grow on me. I'd get used to them. All that good stuff.

I turned around to face the mall traffic. Lots of people walking by had glasses. Yesterday, I wouldn't have even noticed. Maybe it wasn't as big a deal as I was making it out to be.

A howl of pain followed by mocking laughter made me look to the right. And there, headed my way, were Slade Durkin and his two older brothers. They were punching and climbing on one another like animals as they walked.

My stomach seized. I didn't want to deal with King of the Bullies right now.

I glanced inside the store. Mom was still at the register, chattering away with the saleslady. I thought about heading back inside, but another yelp of pain made me look again at the Durkins.

One of his older brothers had Slade's arm twisted behind his back. The other brother laughed and drilled the most violent noogie I'd ever seen into Slade's scalp. People walking by glanced at them but did nothing.

As Slade struggled to get out of his brothers' grip, embarrassment bloomed on his face. And for a moment he wasn't this mean, evil boy who taunted kids in school and had caused me so many problems. He was one of us. Just a kid himself, being tortured by bigger, meaner kids. Even if they were only his brothers.

I pushed myself off the wall and stepped toward them. I had no plan, no clue what I was going to say. I just wanted them to leave Slade alone.

As I got closer, Slade noticed me, and our eyes connected. At first, his cheeks turned red, his shame even deeper now that someone from school had seen *him* getting bullied. He looked from me to his brothers and back again. Then the panic slid from his face.

Confidence rose up inside of me. I was making him feel better already! I was going to be a hero!

"Hey, Norah!" Slade called out. His brothers loosened their grip to look at me. "You were already ugly enough. You didn't need to go and get glasses!"

I flinched and stopped mid-stride. It felt like someone had punched me in the gut. How did bullies always know how to pick the words that would hurt the most?

Slade's brothers threw their heads back in laughter. They released Slade, who then straightened and laughed along with them. As they walked by, he said, "Seriously, Norah. If you were a dinosaur, you'd be a Nerdosaurus rex."

His brothers laughed even harder, snorting and punching each other in the arms. One of them said to Slade proudly, "You're a Danville boy, all right."

What did *that* mean? They all lived in this town, so weren't they automatically Danville boys? But I didn't even care. Tears stung my eyes, and I willed them not to fall down my cheeks.

I didn't know what I was more upset about, that Slade had said I looked ugly . . . or that I'd temporarily mistaken him for a human being.

Chapter 10

The next morning, I felt so depressed I even thought about faking an illness. Though Darcy had done this plenty of times (and attempted to school me in all acts of parental trickery), I had never lied about being sick to my parents. And, despite how much I wanted to hide in my bedroom all day, I wasn't going to start now.

We had a Spanish test, and Mr. Graham's makeup tests are always harder than the real thing. (Probably to discourage the whole faking-sick-on-test-days thing.) I didn't need that stress. On top of that, I was so busy lately with Partners in Crime along with my regular school stuff. Seventh grade seemed like it had double the amount of homework that sixth had. So I sucked it up and went to school.

Strangely, though getting glasses was a big deal to me, most people didn't seem to notice. I got no crazy looks in the hallway, and no one made any mean, Slade-like remarks. Even though I felt as if my whole face had changed, to everyone else I was still regular Norah Burridge.

Between the Spanish test and a pop quiz in English, it was a busy morning, and I barely had time to talk to *anyone*, not even Darcy. She only had a chance to tell me "Cool specs" as we rushed between classes.

I finally got a moment to rest at lunch. When I walked over to our usual spot, I saw Fiona was sitting at the popular table. We'd get her back tomorrow as part of our Share Plan.

I dropped my lunch bag on the table and eyeballed Darcy. She was eating a pudding cup and had two more lined up.

"Three puddings?" I said. "That's your lunch?"

"I can't chew," she answered through a mouthful of liquid chocolate. "It's too sore."

Oh. Bad friend alert. In all my worrying about my own problems, I'd forgotten that Darcy got braces yesterday. And I hadn't even noticed them in any classes or in the halls this morning! I tried for a .

cheery tone. "Well, Zane says the soreness only lasts a day or two."

Then I remembered how all the things my mom had said to try to make me feel better about glasses hadn't worked at all and realized the only thing I could do was be Darcy's friend. I sat beside her and made little circles on her back with my hand. "I'm sorry about the braces," I said gently.

"Sorry?" She wiped the chocolate off her mouth with a napkin. "Don't be sorry. They're awesome!"

Shocked, I stuttered, "Uh — what?"

"The pain stinks, but like you said, that's only for a day or so. Check them out!" She smiled huge, and I really saw the braces for the first time.

They were purple.

My eyes widened. "Purple braces? I didn't know those existed."

"Me neither," Darcy said excitedly. "I thought I'd be stuck with those same metal ones like everyone else. But my mom told me I could get colored ones. This changes everything. These things rock!"

Darcy wore either black or purple every day, and the braces totally matched her tough-chick style. They actually *did* look kind of cool on her!

I wished I felt the same about the new addition to *my* face.

"What's wrong?" she asked, realizing I wasn't as happy as she was.

I filled her in on the Durkin brothers' appearance at the mall and what Slade had said about me looking ugly.

Darcy rolled her eyes. "Slade's such a jerk. He just wanted to impress his older brothers, and you impress a Durkin by being mean. You happened to be in the wrong spot at the wrong time. You are *not* ugly and your glasses look great. I swear."

She held out her fist like a solemn oath. I half-heartedly bumped it. "Thanks," I muttered, but I knew she was just trying to make me feel better. She's my best friend. That's her job.

Darcy knows me well, so she changed the subject. "Tell me all the details about yesterday's investigation," she prodded.

As we wolfed down our lunches, I filled her in on everything, from the lack of leads to the fact that the Old Witch was totally harmless, even sweet.

Darcy settled back into her seat and furrowed her brow. "Really."

I raised my hands. "So we're out of options. I have no idea what to do next."

The bell rang, and we got to our feet.

"Partners in Crime meeting at my house after school," Darcy said, picking up her tray. She leaned toward me and whispered, "I have a theory."

That afternoon, I waited for Darcy at my locker. I held my books in my arms and leaned up against the cool metal, watching kids get ready to leave for the day.

Down the hall, Zane and Maya were walking side by side. They'd have to pass me to get to the exit. I didn't want to stare, so I pretended to gaze straight in front of me, but really my eyes looked left, trying to sneak peeks at them. As they got closer, I realized they were talking in low voices. I strained to hear. Were they talking about whatever Zane's secret was? Dang it, why couldn't I be Spider-Man right now? (Not for shooting webs out of my wrists — that's gross — but for his superhearing.)

Maya seemed to be trying to convince Zane of something. She was pleading with her hands while he had a sheepish, unsure expression on his face. And then he noticed me.

Yep, Zane caught me staring. He stopped walking and his eyes widened. Maya whispered something to him, and he shook his head quickly and started walking faster in my direction.

I straightened up, and every nag my mother ever said ran through my head. *Don't slouch! Pull your shoulders back.* I flattened myself against the locker, and the dial poked me in the back. I winced and lowered my face. *Keep your head up,* Mom's voice said. My thumb nervously went to my mouth. *Don't bite your nails!*

I almost yelled "Fine!" out loud, but thankfully I wasn't completely insane in that moment. Only mildly crazy.

I thought Zane was going to continue to power walk by, but as he got to where I was standing, he slowed. He looked up — right at me — and his face was a little flushed. He gave a shy smile and said, "I like your new glasses, Norah. They look really good."

"Thank you," I managed to say. He smiled again, bigger this time, and continued on his way. Maya gave me a little wave as she passed.

I let out the huge breath I hadn't realized I'd been holding in. I would've taken his words as a compliment, but Zane was probably just being nice. He was easily the kindest boy in Danville Middle School.

Still, my heart was beating like I was on mile twenty-six of a marathon.

My teeny, tiny, atom-size crush on Zane (okay, fine, Milky Way galaxy–size crush) kept me from noticing Fiona until she stood right in front of me.

Fiona gaped. "Oh. My. Fashion. Goddess."

I whipped around to see who was standing behind me. No one. Just the locker. Then I slowly turned back. "Are you making fun of me?" I was more confused than hurt. I'd thought we were past that.

She took another step and examined me closely. I felt like a bug under a microscope.

"I can't believe it," she said. "Why didn't I think of this? It's genius. It's what I was searching for all along!"

I asked, "Are you, like, sleepwalking or something? Because you're making no sense."

"The glasses, you doofus! They're perfect!"

I tilted my head like my dog, Hubble, does when I babble to him and he has no clue what I'm saying.

(Yes, I talk to my dog. It's useful sometimes since he doesn't talk back.)

Fiona, finally realizing my cluelessness, waved her hands excitedly. "You know how I kept saying that your look was missing something but I couldn't put my finger on what it was?"

"It was . . . glasses?"

"Yes! You look so . . . sophisticated."

Now it was my turn to be shocked. I repeated, "Sophisticated?"

"Absolutely. You look older and more confident. Maybe because you're not all squinty and unsure-looking. And this pair you picked out . . ." She paused. "Wait, there's no way you picked these. Who helped you?" She put her hands on her hips like she was insulted I'd asked someone else's fashion advice instead of hers.

"No one. I picked them myself." I didn't want to tell her that I'd practically chosen them at random because I was ready to have a tantrum in the store. Let her think I'd actually made a wise fashion choice on my own for once.

Fiona shook her head in amazement. "Wonderful pick for your face's shape and your hair color." She reached up and loosened my ponytail a little. "And they're versatile with many looks. You're just adorable, Norah Burridge!"

"Wow," I said, feeling truly stunned by all these compliments. "Thanks."

Everyone who'd mentioned my new glasses had told me they looked great (except Slade) — but I hadn't believed them. I'd thought they were all just being nice. Fiona, however, doesn't do "nice" when it comes to fashion. She only knows honesty. So, if she thought the glasses were perfect for me . . . I believed her. I could already feel myself standing taller, feeling more confident.

"Hey," Darcy said, giving me a little hip check as she got to us. "Ready to go?"

"My glasses look great," I told her, my voice giving away my surprise.

"Duh," Darcy said. "I told you that this morning. And at lunch." Then she looked at Fiona, back at me, and said, "But you didn't believe it until *Teen Vogue* over here said it."

Whoops. A little nugget of guilt sat in the pit of my stomach. "Sorry?" I said with a sheepish smile. "She does know a lot about style, though."

"And I also know about time," Fiona butted in. "If we're going to have a Partners in Crime meeting, we should get going."

"You're coming?" Darcy said. Her jaw tightened. Something most people wouldn't notice, but it didn't slip past me.

"Yeah," Fiona said. "Norah invited me along. I'm glad cheering got canceled today. I'm looking forward to chilling with you guys."

"Me . . . too," Darcy said with a small smile.

But the smile didn't reach her eyes.

Chapter 11

I didn't know what Darcy's problem was. Maybe I'd hurt her feelings over the whole glasses thing. But, obviously, Fiona's opinion would matter more than Darcy's when it came to style. Just like if I wanted to buy a new laptop, I'd ask what Darcy thought, not Fiona. And if someone needed to know how many moons Jupiter has, they'd ask me. (At least sixty-five, though we'll probably discover more in time.) The point is, we know about different things.

But I wasn't about to bring it up again, especially now that we were at Darcy's house and she was acting normal again.

Well, normal for her.

"My mom and I baked cupcakes last night," she said, taking the lid off a container.

Fiona and I, seated at the kitchen table, leaned over to look inside. They were chocolate cupcakes with orange icing, plus a layer of black icing threaded across to look like spiderwebs. I smiled. They were *so* Darcy.

Fiona sat back in her chair. "Is it Halloween and I just don't know it?"

I reached in and pulled out two cupcakes, handing one to Fiona. "Just eat it and thank me after. Darcy and her mom make great cupcakes."

Her hostess duties done, Darcy sat down and opened up the black notebook.

"What do we have to add to the case file?" Fiona asked, licking a dot of frosting off her top lip.

"Well," I said. "We can cross off accidental interference. No one else has a baby monitor."

"Not necessarily." Darcy lifted her pencil into the air. "No one has a *baby*."

I carefully peeled the liner off my cupcake. "What's the difference?"

"The baby monitor is pretty cheap, right? Sixteen

bucks? Someone could have bought one knowing Maya would hear the voices. Just to scare her."

I took a big bite and let Darcy's words settle in. So *that* was her theory. It figured she'd go the conspiracy route, but she had a point. You didn't have to have a baby to buy a monitor. And the voices *had* come through only on Saturday nights, when Maya was baby-sitting her brother and therefore would be listening. And the voice or voices were certainly creepy. It wasn't just someone talking about nothing important, which is what accidental interference would probably sound like.

I nodded slowly. "It's a definite possibility. But who would do that?"

"I think we have two strong contenders." Darcy stabbed her finger at the notebook in two places. "Anya and Hunter."

"Hunter, no doubt," I agreed. "He loves messing with people. And he's teased Maya before on walks home from school."

Fiona dabbed at her mouth with a napkin. "But this is a lot more involved than his usual pranks. And I doubt he'd spend his own money on a monitor just to mess with the girl next door."

Darcy tapped the end of her pencil on the table. "Then there's always Anya: Worst Sister Ever. I wouldn't put it past her."

"But Maya insisted Anya was out when she first heard the voices," I said.

"She could've just *told* her she was going out," Fiona said. "Maybe she took the second monitor into the woods, and she and her friends did the spooky voice into it."

"The woods *are* in range," Darcy pointed out.

I scooped the cupcake crumbs into a napkin and balled it up into my hand. Anya *would* know when Maya was home babysitting. When she'd be sitting there watching TV, listening to the monitor. And, from the way I saw her treat Maya, I knew Anya had a mean streak. She was the complete opposite of shy, sweet-natured Maya.

I felt a flash of anger. If someone was doing this on purpose to scare Maya, I wanted to put a stop to it. She didn't deserve to be treated that way.

"But how do we find the evidence?" I said, thinking out loud. "How could we prove it?"

Darcy got a glimmer in her eye. "We catch her in the act."

"Another sleepover?" I said.

Darcy nodded eagerly. "And this time . . . we'll be prepared."

Fiona clapped her hands and bounced in her seat. "Yay! A sleepover! And this time . . . I can come!"

While Darcy stepped out of the kitchen to call Maya and ask if she wanted to do another sleepover stakeout, I opened my daily calendar in the back of my binder. I tried to figure out a game plan for the rest of my week. But the more I looked at everything I had going on, the more stressed I got.

Mr. Mahoney had assigned us a brand-new science project, right when I wanted to start focusing on my social studies project. Plus, Mrs. Haymon, my math teacher, talked to me after class about some state math competition she wanted me to enter. And this was all on top of my regular homework!

I had so much to do, my head was spinning. Fiona was sitting there happily texting away on her phone. I don't know how she kept it together. Chatting with all her friends, cheering, taking the time to make sure her hair and clothes were perfect every day, plus school stuff. Well, she didn't exactly ace the school stuff, but you know. I'm sure she put in *some* effort.

I looked back at my to-do list and tried to prioritize. Then I put my face in my hands and groaned.

"It's *on* like *no* spelled backward!" Darcy cheered, returning to the kitchen, cell phone in hand.

"The sleepover?" Fiona said.

"Yep!" Darcy slid into the seat next to me. "Saturday night at Maya's. We're going to catch Anya . . . or whoever . . . in the act."

I didn't realize I was rubbing my forehead until Darcy said, "What's wrong, stress ball?"

I pointed at my planner and said, "I'm just feeling a little overwhelmed at the moment."

"Is it because of the social studies project?" Darcy waved her hand. "Don't worry about it. We'll work on that this weekend."

"It isn't just one thing," I started to explain.

Darcy's face lit up. "You know what you need? A night of pizza, popcorn, and *Crime Scene: New York.* It's a new episode tonight." She aimed a thumb toward the giant TV in the living room.

My shoulders sagged. "I wish I could, but I don't have time."

Darcy pouted. "What do you have to do?"

"I've done so much Partners in Crime stuff lately, plus I wasted time this week on glasses-induced depression. I have a ton of reading to catch up on and I don't want to fall behind on my homework assignments."

Then I remembered that my parents were planning a Family Movie Night for tonight, too. Ugh! Like I had time for a movie. Not to mention, I hadn't visited my favorite astronomy blog or done any sky-gazing with my telescope in forever. Even my most-loved hobby was suffering!

Darcy must have seen the panic in my eyes, because she put a steady hand on my shoulder and said, "Chill. I can watch the show alone." She opened up her laptop and muttered under her breath, "That's what I usually do anyway."

I didn't have time for one of Darcy's mood swings. Fiona and I stood and grabbed our backpacks, ready to leave. But then Darcy shot a hand out. "Hold up, guys."

"What?" I asked.

"We just got an e-mail about another case!" Darcy sounded all revved up about it.

My backpack felt heavier on my shoulders as I asked, "What does it say?"

She read aloud. "I heard around school that you guys are running this detective agency like it's real. I need your help. Can we meet tomorrow afternoon?" Then Darcy's eyes got even wider.

"Who's it from?" Fiona said.

Darcy looked up at us. "Hunter Fisk."

I wagged a finger in the air. I wasn't going to spend any time helping *that* guy. "No. Ohhhhh, no."

"I know he's a big jerkface," Darcy said. "But aren't you the least bit curious about what he needs help with?"

"No, I'm not," I said honestly. "I'm too busy with everything I have to do and our current case for Maya. He probably just wants us to do something illegal, like get him test answers or something."

"What if he really needs help?" Darcy said.

I gave her a look. Like she cared about helping Hunter Fisk. She just wanted to know what his mystery was — if it even was that.

"I'm not meeting him," I said. "He can solve his own problem."

Fiona and I said good-bye to Darcy and headed out

the front door. I felt a little bit guilty for saying no to Darcy, but I was seriously so stressed out. I had to catch up on all my work. And we had Maya's sleepover to plan for. And it was *Hunter* . . . come on.

"See you later, Fiona," I said and headed toward my house next door.

"Hey, wait a sec," Fiona said. "I was wondering . . . would you let me pick out your clothes for tomorrow?"

I looked at her sideways. "What?"

"With your new glasses and all that, I'd love to style you."

"I'm not your doll," I joked.

"Come on. Just for one day." She gently tugged on my ponytail. "Pleeeeease. Please, please, please, please, please." She hopped in place as she begged.

"Okay, fine, if it will shut you up," I said with a giggle. "Make it quick, though."

"I know, brainiac, you have a *ton* to do."

And then she followed me inside. She may have been skipping.

Chapter 12

Fiona sighed as she flipped through the clothes hanging in my closet. "I feel like an artist who's used to working with oils and paints but was only given a pencil to create a masterpiece."

I threw myself onto a beanbag chair. "This was *your* idea, remember? Besides, I like my clothes. They're comfortable."

A hanger screeched as she pulled another rejected choice aside. "All I'm saying is, it wouldn't kill you to branch out and wear something more *colorful* or *interesting* sometimes." She held up my gray pleated skirt as an example. Then she grinned at me over her shoulder. "Trying new things is good."

"Yeah, yeah," I said in a mocking tone. But I wasn't annoyed. I was actually . . . having fun. Which was strange. Fiona was so different from me, and together we did things that were so different from what I did with Darcy. But different didn't mean bad.

Before I got to know Fiona, I'd always thought of her as superficial and shallow. But it's not that she doesn't care deeply. about anything; it's just that she cares about things that don't interest me. And she always thought of me as just a nerd and . . . well, she still probably thought I was a nerd . . . but we had this sort of mutual respect thing going on now. I liked it.

Fiona pushed all the hangers to the left and let out a gasp. "What do we have here?" She pulled out a short skirt with a flowery print and held it up, her mouth a giant O in surprise.

"My mom bought it," I said.

"Well, that explains why it's so cute," she said. "It's fun and frilly. Love. It." She tossed the skirt at me. "Try it on. With" — she reached back into the closet and pulled out a thin black sweater — "this thing. It'll have to do."

I tried on the outfit while Fiona scrambled on her hands and knees through the shoes that littered the bottom of my closet. "Hey, these boots aren't bad," she said, tossing them over her shoulder.

I put those on, too. And then stood, ready to be judged.

Fiona paced back and forth, tapping the end of her nose. I felt like one of those girls lined up ready to get kicked off a reality show. Finally, after the longest minute ever, she threw her hands into the air. "It's perfect!"

My mouth dropped open. "Really?"

"The skirt is a flirty splash of color, but the black top is sophisticated like your glasses. And the boots tie everything together." Her eyes snapped up to mine. "You'll need to wear black tights tomorrow, though. Please tell me you have tights."

"Yes, I have black tights," I said with a smirk.

"Good." She clapped her hands together. "Now for your hair."

Fiona straightened my hair and made me pinky-swear promise that I wouldn't wash it in the morning, *and* that I'd wear the outfit she'd picked out. I'll admit everything looked great, but it was way too much effort. I didn't know how Fiona went through all that trouble every single morning.

My mom insisted Fiona stay for dinner and Family Movie Night. Despite how much I hadn't wanted to waste time watching a movie, the comedy my dad chose was pretty funny. After Fiona left, I was a speed-reading machine and caught up on a ton of work. I was feeling a lot less stressed when I got to school Thursday morning.

Darcy, however, was not.

She hadn't met me at my locker like most mornings, so I poked my head into our homeroom and found she was already there. I slid into my seat in front of her. She had a book open but didn't seem to be reading it, and she was scowling more than usual.

"How was *Crime Scene: New York?*" I asked, pushing my glasses up on my nose. I was still getting used to them.

Darcy shrugged. "Fine."

Huh. Usually she went into elaborate detail, telling me every twist and turn of the episode.

She looked up at me sharply. "What did you do last night?"

"Family Movie Night. You know how that goes." The thought occurred to me that once Fiona had decided to stay for the movie, I should have called Darcy and invited her over, too. But she probably would've rather watched *Crime Scene: New York* anyway. So it was for the best that I hadn't.

Darcy snorted and returned to pretend-reading her book.

"Is something wrong?" I asked.

"Yeah," she mumbled. "That outfit."

I looked down and smoothed out the skirt with my hands. I'd felt pretty good about the outfit when I put it on that morning. Granted, it wasn't really me, but it was fun to try something new every now and then, I guess. Now, though, I felt self-conscious.

I turned away from Darcy and opened a notebook.

Fiona strolled in and immediately checked to see if I was wearing the clothes she'd picked out. Then she gave me a thumbs-up and took her seat one row over.

I hated this silent treatment thing Darcy and I were doing to each other. And I didn't even know why it was happening. I forced a happy tone into my voice as I turned to my BFF. "So do you want to hang out after school? Do our homework together?"

Her face changed then. The mad look started to go away. But her eyes flashed, as if she remembered something.

"Yeah, sure," she said. "I'll meet you out at the bike rack."

I smiled and turned back around in my seat. Everything was going to be fine. Darcy was just moody sometimes, that's all. I accepted that like she accepted the days when I turned into a stress ball.

That's what best friends do.

At lunch, Darcy, Fiona, and I made plans for our Saturday night sleepover, part two.

"I got a new toy to bring with us," Darcy said, eyes alight. "I'll show you guys when we get to Maya's house."

"Why does that statement scare me?" Fiona said.

I laughed. "I saw Maya in the hall earlier. She's happy we're coming. I think the time she's spent with us is helping to bring her out of her shell." I was happy about that. Maya was really nice. She just needed to put herself out there more.

Fiona waggled her eyebrows and said, "Speaking of people being shy . . ."

I turned to see what she was looking at. Zane was standing at the condiments table. He looked over at me, and my eyes shot back down to my plate. Why did he always catch me staring at him?

"He sure is taking his time picking out a ketchup packet," Darcy said.

"He totally wants to talk to you," Fiona added.

Then they both started giggling like idiots.

"Stop it," I whispered. "You're going to embarrass me."

"Oh, relax and go talk to him," Fiona said.

Easy for her to say. This boy stuff came natural to her. It was painful for me. "What would I even say?"

"Oh, I don't know. . . . You could start with 'hi,'" Fiona said sarcastically.

I gave her a look and she said, "Come on. You're all dressed up today. It's like fate."

Fate? Yeah, right. My logical mind does not compute that. Plus, I'd forgotten I was wearing the "special" outfit. Now I wanted to hide under the table.

"You could tell him about the sleepover," Darcy suggested. "Maybe he'd offer to keep an eye out for anything suspicious in the neighborhood."

Huh. Now, *that* was something reasonable.

"Oh! He's looking at us! He's looking!" Fiona said, waving her hands. "Go, go!"

I decided to just get up and talk to him before Fiona's head exploded.

I turned and found Zane already walking toward me. We met halfway and I positioned myself so he wasn't facing Darcy and Fiona. I was. He didn't need to see them staring at us the whole time, which I *knew* they were going to do.

"Hey," I said, sounding desperately uncool.

"Hey, Norah." He bit his bottom lip. "You look nice. With your glasses and those clothes and stuff . . . you look . . . older."

I looked down at myself and back up again, blushing. "Um, thanks."

"Though I like your regular clothes just as much," he added.

And that might have been the best compliment I'd ever gotten.

I grinned and then he smiled and, I'm telling you, his smile was brighter than a supernova. (For you non-astronomers out there, that's *very* bright.)

I shuffled my feet nervously. "So, um, I wanted to let you know that we're doing another sleepover on your street this weekend. At Maya's."

"Are you still trying to figure out that weird voice?" he asked quietly.

"Yeah. We're hoping to get to the bottom of it Saturday night."

Darcy was making kissy-faces behind Zane's back. I was glad she liked crime shows so much, because she was going to star in one after I murdered her.

Zane suddenly turned serious. "Be careful out there, Norah. Don't go wandering in the woods behind the houses."

"Why not?" I asked. Despite the obvious: Woods are creepy.

He fiddled with the ketchup packet in his hand. "I've heard stuff out there sometimes. At night. It could be animals, but who knows. Just . . . be careful, okay?"

His eyes had this earnest look to them. Like he

really did care. He was . . . worried about me. I'd never really fully grasped the meaning of the word *swoon* until that moment.

I felt my cheeks reddening again as I said, "Okay, I will."

Chapter 13

After the last bell, I grabbed my stuff from my locker and headed out to the bike rack, where Darcy had told me to meet her. She was already there, but she wasn't alone.

Hunter stood next to her.

He kept pushing the sleeves of his flannel shirt up his forearms, then they'd fall again, and he'd push them back up. And he shuffled from foot to foot while his eyes darted all around. Why was he acting so weird . . . and nervous?

"Hey," Darcy said as I came up to them. "You're here."

"Yeah . . ." I was too polite to add *And what's he*

doing here? My eyes went to Hunter for an explanation and he — for the first time in his entire life — gave me a weak smile. My mind took a moment to process that, and then I figured out what was going on.

Hunter was being nice because he thought I was going to help him with something.

Darcy had replied to his e-mail.

I glared at Darcy. "I thought we'd agreed we were too busy to take on another case."

"*You* said that." Darcy crossed her arms. "I didn't agree."

My mouth opened and closed silently. She'd gone ahead and answered his e-mail, then agreed to meet him, and hadn't told me. And then also didn't happen to mention when we'd made plans to meet after school that Hunter would be with her!

Through tightly pursed lips, I hissed, "I thought we made Partners in Crime decisions together."

Darcy cocked her head. "Funny, that's what I've been wondering lately, too."

I winced. *What did* that *mean?*

Hunter stepped in between us. "Will you guys stop fighting, please? You're starting to sound like Slade and me lately."

I looked up at Hunter and noticed there was a bit of hurt in his eyes. He and Slade were fighting, too? What was up with all the BFFs at Danville Middle School?

Out of curiosity, I asked, "What's wrong with you and Slade?"

Hunter shrugged like he didn't care, but his face betrayed him. "Slade doesn't have much time for me anymore."

Darcy snorted, but her face was hidden by Hunter's huge frame, so I didn't know if she was happy about Hunter and Slade's problem or what.

"Just look at the note and then you can decide if you want to take on my case," Hunter pleaded. "Please. It'll only take one second."

Whoa. Hunter Fisk just used the word *please*. I exhaled loudly. "Fine. What note?"

He reached into the back pocket of his jeans. "It showed up in my locker yesterday. It's small enough that someone could just push it through the vent. It's . . . um . . . threatening."

Well, it shouldn't be a huge surprise that Hunter had made someone mad, I thought. He probably made enemies every day. But who would have the guts to stand up to him? I held out my hand, and he slid the note onto my palm.

Only two words were on it, in large block text: YOU'RE NEXT.

I tried to swallow, but my throat was suddenly bone dry. I hadn't been prepared for something so simple and . . . creepy. I'd been expecting something like: *Leave me alone or I'll tell Principal Plati!*

This note might not have anything to do with Hunter's favorite hobby of bullying kids. This might be something completely different. And the "next" part implied that it was something already in progress, with other victims.

"Was there anything else?" I asked.

He ran a hand through his shaggy hair. "Not really. There's just some weird design on the other side."

I flipped it over. The swirly design looked familiar. Very familiar. Then I realized where I'd seen it before, and my stomach dropped.

The same design had been on the note I'd found on the ground behind Maya's house. I slid my backpack off my shoulder and started frantically searching through it.

"What's wrong?" Darcy asked, stepping around Hunter to stand beside me. "What are you doing?"

I pulled the scrap of paper from the bottom of my bag and smoothed out the creases. Then I held it up to show Darcy and Hunter. "I found this on the ground the night we were outside Maya's house, searching for that mysterious voice."

Hunter's eyes widened. "It's the same logo."

Darcy took it out of my hand and brought it up close to her face. "Why didn't you tell me about this?"

I drew in a shaky breath. "I figured it didn't mean anything. It's just a swirly design."

She lowered the note. "Have you looked good and hard at it since you've gotten your glasses?"

"No . . . why?" She handed it back and I took a longer look. It *wasn't* just a meaningless design. It was three letters drawn in elaborate cursive and linked together with decorative swirls. I'd never noticed before.

"The letters *TDB*?" I said.

"That's what it looks like to me," Darcy said.

"What does *TDB* mean?" Hunter asked us.

Darcy shook her head. "I don't know. It could be someone's initials."

"But whose?" Hunter demanded. "And what am I 'next' for?"

I felt a pang of intrigue mixed with fear. I thought about the words Maya had told us she'd first heard on the monitor: someone saying "Get him" and then a scream. And then what we'd heard . . . someone begging for help . . . someone scared. And this symbol, design, logo, had been on the ground by her house. Now Hunter had gotten the same note with a message saying he was next.

Something added up but didn't.

"Do you think the voices on the baby monitor have to do with this note?" I asked, holding up Hunter's note for Darcy.

"Maybe," Darcy said slowly.

Hunter gave us a look that was part smug and part hopeful. "So you'll take on my case now, right?"

I exchanged a look with Darcy and answered Hunter, "Yeah. Something's going on and —"

"And you might be in danger," Darcy finished for me.

I knew Darcy and I were thinking the same thing. We hadn't picked up some innocent conversation from someone else's baby monitor. And now it didn't even look as if this was staged to scare Maya. We'd stumbled upon something real. And dangerous. Something was going on out there, in the dark, in the woods.

This changed everything.

Chapter 14

The only good thing about discovering that the voice in the woods might be something dangerous was that Darcy and I weren't fighting anymore. Not that we were *fighting* before. But you know. The sleepover became the top priority.

Mom pulled into the Doshis' driveway Saturday night just as Darcy's mom and Fiona's dad were pulling out. We'd all arrived at basically the same time.

Mom looked at the pile of stuff on my lap. "You have everything?"

A mixture of emotions ran through me: excitement, anticipation, and even a little bit of fear. I hefted my overnight bag up over one shoulder and held the sleeping bag with my arms. "Yep! See you in the morning." I pushed the car door with my foot.

Mom called out, "Remember, if for any reason you want to come home, just give us a call."

"I would, but I don't have a cell phone," I said with a glint in my eye.

Mom chuckled. "I'm sure the Doshis have a house phone. Nice try, though."

I was convinced that one of these tries, someday, was going to work.

Maya swung open the front door as I approached the house. She waved me in. "Come on. Everyone's in the kitchen!"

I dropped my bags on the floor and slipped out of my sneakers, then followed Maya into the kitchen. Fiona, Darcy, and Anya were seated around the table. Rishi was in one of those baby bouncy seats, kicking and cooing. Mrs. Doshi was searching through every drawer in the room.

Maya whispered, "She can't find her keys."

I knew that dance well. My father did it all the time. Finally, Mrs. Doshi lifted a newspaper from the counter, said, "There they are!" and did a little victory shimmy.

Then she turned to us. "Okay, girls, I'm heading to the restaurant. Let's see. . . . Anya." She pointed at her oldest daughter. "Rishi has already had his dinner. Just play with him for about an hour and then put him to bed."

Anya smiled sweetly. "Of course." She seemed a lot nicer tonight.

"Maya," Mrs. Doshi continued, "what would you and your friends like for dinner?"

"I already told you, Mom. We ordered a pizza."

Mrs. Doshi made a face. "Are you sure you wouldn't rather have something from the restaurant? I can pack you up a nice meal and bring it back here —"

"And then head back to the restaurant? That's too much work for you." Maya pointed at the window. "Look, Mom, it's dark already. This is the restaurant's busiest night. Dad needs you. Don't worry about us."

I nodded and smiled. I appreciated that Mrs. Doshi was trying to be a good host, but I'd really rather have the pizza. And the house to ourselves so we could kick this stakeout into high gear.

"All right. Have fun, girls!" Mrs. Doshi gave Maya and Anya light kisses on the tops of their heads, waved at us, and left.

But as soon as the front door shut, everything changed.

Anya slammed her hands on the table so loudly I jumped in my seat.

"This has to stop," she hissed.

Maya slouched down in her chair. "What are you talking about?"

Anya stood so she towered over us. She glared at Maya. "This is two Saturdays in a row I had to stay in and babysit Rishi because of you."

Maya said weakly, "I babysat him both Friday nights so you could go out. It's only fair. I do Fridays, you do Saturdays. It's the same thing."

I wanted to high-five Maya for standing up for herself. Though her tone could've used a little more strength, it was a good start.

"It's *not* the same thing," Anya retorted. "I have parties to go to, friends to go out with. You're just pretending to have friends."

I felt a flare of anger, and I knew Darcy and Fiona did, too. Darcy stood up and crossed her arms over her chest. I was sure she was going to lash out at Anya in a way that could possibly get us in trouble, so I grabbed her arm.

"We're not imaginary," I told Anya, my tone cool.

Anya's eyes cut to me. "But I'm sure you didn't come over here for Maya's sparkling personality. Did she pay you or something? Offer to do your homework?"

I felt heat on my neck, working its way up my cheeks as I got angrier. Even though we were only here for a case, that didn't mean we weren't becoming friends with Maya along the way.

Fiona piped up, "We *are* her friends. Maya has plenty of friends. You'd know how nice she was if you bothered to chat with her instead of ordering her around."

I wanted to hug Fiona.

Anya snorted. "Yeah, right. Maya had no friends in our old town and she'll have none in this one, either." And with that she stood, the chair scraping loudly against the floor. She picked Rishi up out of his bouncy seat and brought him upstairs, stomping all the way.

Maya stared at the floor in silence. I didn't know if she was depressed, embarrassed, or both.

"Wow, you guys weren't kidding about Anya being nasty," Fiona said, shaking her head. She looked at Maya with pity in her eyes, and I knew she was thinking of her own little sister as she said, "You're her sister. How could she treat you that way?"

"Anya's a bully," Darcy said. "And even bullies have brothers and sisters."

I thought about Slade in the mall with his older brothers. He'd learned how to bully by being bullied himself. But Maya was proof that it didn't have to end up that way. Anya treated her cruelly, but Maya was still one of the nicest girls around. I vowed to make sure Maya always knew she had friends. In school, at home, whenever she needed us.

"Don't let Anya get you down, Maya," I said. "You have us."

Maya looked up with sad eyes. "You guys might have been right all along."

"About what?" Darcy asked.

"That Anya might be the one doing this. When she said she was going out with her friends that night, it might have been her and her friends outside somewhere making creepy voices into another monitor, knowing I'd be listening, just to scare me." She let out a long sigh. "We bicker and stuff. She's not the world's best sister. But I never thought she'd do something as mean as that."

"It might not be her," I said, adding silently, *It might be something dangerous.*

"Why?" Maya asked, glancing from me to Darcy to Fiona. "Did you guys get any new leads?"

Darcy filled her — and Fiona — in on the note Hunter got with the TDB design, which matched the paper I'd found on the night of our first sleepover.

"Does TDB mean anything to you?" I asked Maya, showing her the two matching notes.

Maya scrunched up her nose. "No. I've never heard of it."

Whatever or whoever TDB was, at that moment, I hoped it had nothing to do with Anya. Because I didn't want to see the hurt on Maya's face if Anya was the guilty one.

"Don't worry," Darcy said confidently. "We'll get to the bottom of this tonight. We're prepared this time. We won't start to fall asleep or have the TV on too loud. We're going to be fully awake, quiet, listening, and ready."

Right at that moment, a crunch of gravel came from outside. My head snapped up. Then another sound came, like a heavy footstep. We all stiffened. I put my finger to my lips, telling everyone to keep quiet.

Another noise . . . a kind of shuffling.

"Where is that coming from?" Fiona whispered.

"It sounds like someone's outside but in the front," I said. Strange. I'd always assumed the person messing with us would be lurking around the back of the house, near the woods, not out in front, facing the street, where he or she could be seen.

And it couldn't have been Anya, because we would've seen her walk out the front door.

Reading my thoughts, Darcy asked, "Is there any way Anya could've snuck out? Do you have a back door?"

Maya nodded. "Maybe she could have tiptoed downstairs and gone out the back."

"Maybe it's just an animal scurrying out there?" Fiona said hopefully.

A heavy footfall came, from closer to the door, followed by an "oomph."

That was no animal. Squirrels don't trip and say "oomph."

Darcy dashed to the front door and we all followed. My heart hammered in my chest as Darcy rose on her tiptoes and squinted through the peephole.

"Do you see anything?" I asked.

"Yeah, it's a person. But I can't see all of them. They're looking down at something in their hand." Darcy took a step back and reached for the handle. "Time for us to give someone a little surprise."

We all huddled together, touching shoulders, a giant wall of angry yet frightened twelve-year-olds ready to give whoever wanted to scare us a scare of their own. Darcy turned the knob and yanked the door inward as hard and quickly as she could.

There *was* a person standing there. Not Anya.

Not anyone we knew.

Chapter 15

The stranger screamed.

Then we screamed.

(Hey, when you yank open a door and some dude is standing there with his fist raised in the air, and he starts yelling . . . it's just a reflex to yell back.)

Then I took in his red jacket, matching hat, and the box he held in one hand while the other seemed frozen in the air, ready to knock on the door that was now wide open.

"Girls!" I yelled. "It's only the pizza guy!"

They all stopped screaming, then the pizza guy stopped screaming. The fist he'd meant to use for knocking on the door now clutched his poor heart.

Between ragged breaths, he said, "One . . . large . . . half plain, half . . . pepperoni?"

"Yes, that's us," Darcy said apologetically. "Sorry about the aggressive door opening. We're, uh, really hungry."

"Ten bucks," he replied, obviously wanting no small talk. I didn't blame him for wanting to get out of there, and away from the creepy four girls staring at him as quickly as possible.

Mrs. Doshi had given Maya fifteen dollars. She held it out and said, "Keep the change."

He didn't even say good-bye. And almost ran away, tripping again on one of the steps and letting out another "oomph."

We attacked the pizza like we hadn't eaten in a week. No talking, just noshing, until all that was left in the box were crumbs and grease. Mystery solving makes girls hungry, I guess.

I leaned back in the chair and patted my full belly.

Darcy did the same. "That was fanny-tastic."

Fiona daintily dabbed at her mouth with a napkin.

"So what do we do now?" Maya asked, looking eager.

"Sit here and digest," I moaned.

Darcy sat up straight, her eyes sparkling. "How about I show you my new toy?"

"Oh!" Fiona gave a little clap. "I forgot about that. Let's see it."

Darcy wiped her hands with a napkin and went into the corner where we'd tossed our overnight bags. She unzipped hers and pulled out a bunch of items. "Flashlights," she called out, holding them up. "And . . . these babies."

With a flourish, she lifted up a pair of heavy-looking binoculars that were like nothing I'd ever seen.

Maya's eyes widened. "Are those night-vision goggles?"

Darcy beamed. "They sure are. No one can hide from us now. Even in the dark."

"Are they real?" Fiona asked.

Darcy nodded proudly. "You bet."

I reached out and held the night goggles for a second. They were super heavy. I couldn't help but smile. Darcy and her spy gear. "Where did you get them?" I asked.

"Remember last month when my mom and I flew to California to visit my cousin? They were in the *SkyMall!*"

"That catalog that's in all the seats?" Fiona said.

"Yeah! Turns out it's full of surveillance stuff. It was like a dream come true." She took the goggles back from me and held them in her arms like a baby. "I knew they'd come in handy someday. They'll definitely get some use tonight!"

Fiona went to her bag and started rummaging through it. "I brought equipment, too."

I scrunched up my forehead. What could Fiona have brought for a sleepover stakeout?

She whipped out a pink cosmetics case and said with delight, "Makeover time!"

Darcy's jaw almost hit the floor. Then she spoke slowly, "We're . . . on . . . a . . . spy . . . mission."

Fiona put a hand on her hip. "Hey, we have to do *something* to pass the time. And I can do makeup quietly."

Midnight came and we all were wearing lip gloss — even Darcy — and had our nails done. Fiona's were pink, mine were blue, Maya's were red. Miraculously, Darcy had agreed to have hers painted purple, though she wouldn't move from her post even while they were being done. She'd had the goggles on all night and stared out the window, waiting to catch our villain in the act.

But now we were all makeupped out and getting tired, though we needed to stay awake.

Darcy let out an impatient groan. "This is around the time we heard the voice last week. When is it going to happen?"

I felt the same way. I didn't want this whole night to be a bust. My hand went to my mouth in an attempt to stifle a giant yawn.

"How about a game of Would You Rather?" Fiona suggested.

That could be fun. I went first. "Would you rather be able to read minds or have visions?"

Maya said, "Read minds! That would rule."

"Now someone else ask a question," I said.

A snicker came from Darcy's darkened corner of the room. "Would you rather eat dog poop or a live bee?"

"Eww!" Fiona wrinkled her nose in distaste. "That's too disgusting. New question."

Darcy laughed. "Okay. Would you rather be rich and ugly or poor and hot?"

Fiona gasped. "Oh, that's so hard! Maybe rich and

ugly because I could always cover up my ugly with designer outfits."

Darcy and I rolled our eyes at each other in the darkness, and smiled. Then I searched my mind for a question with a little more depth. But before I could open my mouth, Fiona asked, "Would you rather have one best friend or a bunch of not-as-close friends?"

Darcy quickly said, "One best friend." She hesitated, looking straight at me, then said, "I feel like —"

But she didn't finish her sentence. The monitor had started to crackle.

Chapter

16

My chest tightened. We all scrambled over to the monitor and circled around it.

A voice pushed through the crackling. "Come on . . . this . . . thing . . ." Static hissed for a long moment, then the voice came back again. "Please . . . help me . . ."

The voice sent a trail of ice down my spine. Not just the words, but the tone. The person was panicked and scared. This wasn't a prank. If it was, the person on the other end deserved an acting award.

"I think it's a guy," Darcy whispered.

"Yeah, a boy," Maya added.

We all leaned in closer as if that would make the monitor reveal its secrets.

"Please . . . is anyone out there?" Crackle. Hiss. "I'm hurt."

I bolted to my feet. "We have to go out there."

"Wait." Darcy shot out a hand and held my arm. "What if it's a trap? From TDB?"

She had a good point. But I wasn't going to sit inside here and do nothing while someone out there begged for help. I stared into her eyes. "We *have* to check it out." And she nodded because she knew it was the right thing to do.

Fiona and Maya were still huddled on the floor. "Us, too?" Fiona asked sheepishly.

"Yes," Darcy said. "The more people we have, the quicker we can find this person."

Fiona and Maya shared a look and then slowly stood. We each grabbed a flashlight from Darcy's bag of tricks. Darcy had the goggles up on her forehead, ready to pull them down over her eyes when needed. We slipped into our sneakers as quickly as possible and ran outside.

Utter darkness was creepy enough, but it was even spookier with four flashlights bouncing around the gloom, casting shadows over the trees at the edge of the woods. A shudder ran through my body.

I told myself to be calm. I thought about Zane nearby in his house. I cast my eyes up at the thing that relaxed me most — the night sky — and gasped.

Darcy was immediately at my side. "What is it? What did you see?"

She was probably hoping for a giant clue, but it was much less dramatic than that. "I just . . ." I could barely find the words. "The stars have never looked so clear to me before."

It was like my whole life I'd been sky-gazing through a dirty telescope. Now someone had cleaned the lens.

"Glasses aren't so bad now, are they?" Darcy said. I didn't have to see her to know she was smiling.

"Yeah," I agreed. This moment alone was worth getting glasses.

"You guys," Fiona said nervously, bringing me back to Earth.

"What?" Maya whispered.

"I'm kind of scared. I feel like we're being watched."

I scanned the yard in a slow circle. There were many places to hide. Behind a bush, around a corner, not to mention in the trees. Anyone could be out there. And we didn't even know who or what TDB was.

"Did someone just go into the woods?" Darcy said, her voice trembling. "I think I see someone standing in the woods. No, wait, it's just a tree."

"Dude, you're creeping me out," I said, rubbing my arms against the chill.

"I'm creeping myself out," Darcy replied.

"I don't think we should be out here," Maya whispered.

Fiona nodded. "Let's go back in." Then she covered her mouth with her hand as a stream of giggles leaked out. Darcy raised one eyebrow.

"It's a nervous laugh thing," I explained.

But, no, I'd already decided we weren't going back in. Not when we'd gotten this far. And not when someone out there might need help. "Come on, guys," I said. "Nothing actually scary has happened. We're just freaking ourselves out."

Where this bravery came from, I didn't know. I wished I could bottle it and save it for class presentations. Public speaking: Now that's scary stuff.

I took charge. "Everyone search. Look for a person or some equipment that could transmit, like another monitor or a walkie-talkie or radio of some kind. Remember to look with your eyes *and* your ears." I started pointing. "Maya, you take the front yard. Fiona, you take the sides. Darcy, look all around the backyard."

"Where are you going to look?" Darcy said.

I held out my hand. "Give me the goggles. I'm checking the woods."

Maybe it was the new confidence my glasses had given me. Maybe it was impatience and wanting to know what was going on. I didn't know for sure why, but I was filled with a clear and sudden sense of courage.

Darcy handed me the goggles. "Be safe."

The girls all ran off to search their assigned areas. And I took my first step into the woods. They were darker than dark. Even the light of the moon didn't help much. Had I made a mistake? I knew I could always shout over to my friends if need be.

With trembling hands, I slid on the night-vision goggles. Thankfully they were big enough to fit over my glasses. And suddenly the air around me turned from deep black to an eerie green. I looked over my shoulder toward the yard and could see Darcy examining the back deck. She was only a green blur, but bright in the darkness. This was good. No one could hide from me.

If someone was out in those woods, I'd find them.

Dried twigs and dead leaves snapped and crackled under my shoes as I walked deeper into the woods. With each step, I scanned left and right, my widened eyes looking for any sign that I wasn't alone. Night bugs buzzed, and I swatted at something that flew too close to my face.

A sound cut through the air.

A sob? A soft cry?

I listened, keeping still. A breeze picked up, shaking the tree branches. Their dying leaves dropped down around me like falling snow. And on the wind came a word.

"Help. . . ."

My stomach clenched. I spun in the direction of the voice and charged ahead. My feet were trampling the ground, making all sorts of noise.

I stopped to get my bearings and the voice called out, "I'm over here! Please!"

It was clear now that the voice was young and male. And, though he couldn't see me coming, he could hear me. And he desperately needed help.

I came around two large, thick trees and skidded to a stop.

I adjusted the night-vision goggles to make sure what I was seeing was real.

Fear slithered around me like a snake.

Darcy may have been right. I might have just fallen into a trap.

Chapter 17

I shoved the goggles up on my forehead and pulled the flashlight out of my pocket. I needed to see this in bright light. I flicked on the switch and aimed it onto Slade Durkin.

From his position, lying on the ground, he looked up at me. His eyes were wet and shiny. With my flashlight blaring in his face, I could clearly see him, but he couldn't see who I was. Still, he wasn't surprised that a shadow with a flashlight was standing over him in the dark woods. It was as if he'd been expecting me.

But if I'd just fallen into a trap, I would've expected a smug look on his face. He would've jumped up and yelled, "Gotcha," and then his older brothers would've jumped out from behind the other trees.

But none of that happened.

Slade looked up, red glassy eyes squinting against the harsh glare of the light. Then he sniffled and said, "I'm out of the group. I don't want to be one of the Danville boys anymore. I quit."

The Danville boys . . .

A shiver ran down my spine, and everything clicked into place.

In the mall, when Slade had said those cruel things to me, his older brothers proudly told him he was a true Danville boy. And hadn't Mrs. Wolfson said something about those Danville boys daring each other to bang on her door?

"TDB," I said aloud. "It stands for The Danville Boys."

Slade jerked backward, surprised by my voice. "Who is that?"

"Who were you expecting?" I countered.

He put his hand up to shield his eyes from my flashlight. "Norah Burridge? Is that you? Can you help me up? I twisted my ankle real bad. I can't walk."

"Answer my question first," I demanded. I liked having a bit of power over Slade for once. "Who are The Danville Boys?"

He sighed. "If I tell you, will you help me get out of here?"

"Yes," I promised. I was so excited that I had put it all together, I wanted to run back to Maya's yard and tell everyone. But I had to get to the bottom of this first.

"TDB is kind of like a secret society," Slade explained, wincing as he shifted a little on the ground. "You can get picked to join once you hit seventh grade, but you have to pass certain tests before you're a full member."

And his older brothers were clearly members. "What do they make you do?" I asked.

"Scary things, stuff to test your courage."

"Like what?"

He hesitated, apparently not wanting to spill *all* the society's secrets.

"I can walk away and leave you here," I said, taking a step back. "I don't owe you anything after the way you've treated me." Part of me felt bad saying that — Slade did look so scared and alone. But I wanted answers.

He put his hands up in a begging gesture. "Okay,

okay. I'll tell you." He took a deep breath. "First, I got a note saying I was 'next.'"

Just like Hunter's note.

He continued. "A couple weeks after that, I got another note, saying I had to meet TDB at a certain time and place. I went and they told me about the society and how I had been chosen, but I had to pass the tests to prove my worth. The first test was easy . . . knock on the Old Witch's door."

I shook my head. Poor Mrs. Wolfson.

"Then, another night, I had to steal a lawn ornament from someone's yard. Some gnome thing."

I remembered Maya's neighbor, his extensive garden gnome collection, and the spot that looked like one was missing.

"Then everyone for their last week has to pass the final test alone. Tonight was my night."

"What's the final test?" I asked.

"The Danville Boys blindfold you and walk you out somewhere. You don't know where you are. Then they leave you."

I gasped. "That's awful!" Even for *this* group of bullies.

"It's not that bad," Slade said. "They leave a walkie-talkie with you in case of emergency."

For the first time, I noticed the abandoned walkie-talkie lying on the ground beside him. Another shiver of realization went through me. So there had been other boys. But always the walkie-talkie.

"Why didn't you ask them for help when you hurt your ankle?" I asked.

He looked down. "I did. No one answered." He added sadly, "I tried every channel. Something must be wrong with it. That's why I got so scared and started acting . . . not so brave."

I didn't know why I was about to try to make Slade Durkin feel better, but I couldn't help it. "Slade, it's not that you weren't brave. They did it to you on purpose."

He tilted his head. "What do you mean?"

"Darcy, Fiona, and I have been helping Maya out with a case. For the last few Saturday nights, she's picked up scary voices on the baby monitor in her house." I pointed in the direction I thought Maya's house was.

"Saturday nights is when TDB does their final tests," Slade said.

"Yeah, and each night we've heard some poor kid in the woods, all alone and scared, begging for anyone to help him."

"Not just me?" Slade asked.

"No," I said. "It must be part of the test . . . to scare you as much as possible. They give you the walkie-talkie, but they either shut theirs off or they listen to you begging for help and leave you alone anyway."

Slade's face distorted. He looked crushed. "They'd do that?"

I opened my arms, gesturing to the woods around us. "They just did."

A twig snapped somewhere behind me. I stopped and listened quietly.

Were those the sounds of footsteps?

I spun in a slow circle with the flashlight, but the bouncing glow lit up only small areas. I slipped it back into my pocket and pulled the night-vision goggles back down over my eyes to get a fuller view.

"What are you doing?" Slade said, his voice high and tight now that he was plunged once again into darkness.

But not me. I saw everything in that eerie shade of green. As the sounds grew louder, my breaths started coming faster. My legs wanted to run, but I couldn't leave Slade alone.

From behind a tree, a blur zoomed toward me like a green ghost.

"Don't worry," a menacing voice said. "We always come back."

Chapter
18

I gasped and pushed the night-vision goggles up on my forehead. TDB was here.

Or at least two members. I recognized them as Slade's older brothers and knew them only from their height difference.

How sweet that they'd eventually come back for their brother. But in the meantime, he'd hurt his ankle and been scared nearly to death all alone out there in the dark woods.

I knelt down beside Slade and pulled his arm around my shoulder. I must have looked like the Queen of All Dorks with the night-vision goggles on top of my head, but I didn't care. All I cared about was getting out of there.

"Let's go," I said. "I'm going to try to pull you up."

Slade was twice my size, but between his one good leg and all the strength I could muster, I got him to his feet.

"What do we have here?" one of the brothers snarled. They shined their flashlights in our faces.

I tried to look confident, but inside I was trembling all over. I could barely breathe. I remembered the last time Slade needed to get out of a bad situation with his brothers. He'd insulted me to divert their attention. Would he sacrifice me again now?

"Leave us alone, jerks," Slade said.

"Oh, look who came to Slade's rescue," the taller brother said mockingly. "The Nerdosaurus from the mall."

"Don't call her that!" Slade snapped.

"Ooohhh . . . is she your girlfriend now?" the shorter one teased.

Slade slipped his arm from around my shoulder and leaned his weight against a tree. "No," he snapped, glaring at the guys. "But she had the guts to come out here in the woods in the dark when she heard my voice asking for help on the walkie-talkie. So that makes her better than you guys."

I felt something like a flush of pride come over me.

They moved in closer, and one punched Slade in the shoulder. "Come on, wimp. You know it's all part of the test."

"The torture, you mean," I said.

They ignored me. "Come on, Slade. You can laugh with us when your pal Hunter is out here doing the same thing in a couple weeks."

Slade's face twisted in anger and pain. "It's one thing to pull pranks or play scary games together. It's another thing completely to abandon someone when they're hurt. My ankle's busted." He pointed down at his foot. "The society ends now. You're done."

They moved in closer. The taller one said, "There's two of us here. And one and a half of you."

Half?! I'm only a half? My blood was boiling.

The boy growled, "So we say *you're* done."

And now my blood turned to ice. What were they going to do? I stepped backward until I hit a tree.

And then a voice rang out in the darkness. "Learn to count, losers!"

Darcy stepped forward, flashlight held high. "One!"

Maya's small voice said, "Two."

Fiona yelled, "Three!"

Then from behind them came Zane and Hunter.

Zane said, "And we're four and five. So now *you're* outnumbered."

"Oh, h-hey, Hunter," the short brother stammered. "You're invited to join TDB, too. You don't want to be on the side of those geeks. Come join us."

"Slade is my best friend," Hunter said furiously. "And you left him here, hurt."

"But we came back for him," the tall one said. "It was all in fun. Come on. All the cool older boys are in TDB. You have to join or you'll have no friends."

"That's not true," I said. I pushed myself off the tree and stood beside Darcy, Fiona, and Maya. I'd never been so happy to see them. "Look at us. We're not all in the same group. We couldn't be more different. But we're all friends. And no one forced us to scare or hurt each other to join our little gang."

"Yeah!" Fiona yelled, clapping my shoulder.

"She's right," Slade said. "Hunter'll always have my back. I don't need TDB."

The tall brother snarled, "Fine. Don't join. Be a loser." He slapped the shorter brother's chest. "We're out of here."

"Good luck with your secret society after we tell Principal Plati about it Monday," Zane said.

They stopped mid-stride. "You can't do that," the tall one said, his eyes widening. "He'll tell all the parents and teachers! The Danville Boys will be broken up! It's tradition. It's been passed down from grade to grade for years."

Zane glanced at Darcy and me, unsure.

Darcy whispered, "We *could* tell on them and have TDB broken up. *Or* we could force them to change and get something out of it."

"Like what?" Zane said.

Darcy shrugged and looked at Fiona, Maya, and me for ideas. Suddenly, my mind whirred with a wonderful thought.

I cocked my head. "Then how about a deal?"

"What kind of deal?" the tall one asked with suspicion in his voice.

"We won't tell on TDB in exchange for two things. One — no more hazing. If you invite someone to join the society, you can still make them do scavenger hunts and stuff like that, but never make them feel like they're in danger."

He groaned. "Fine. And?"

I smiled. "And tomorrow you're all going to come prepared to work."

"What kind of work?" the short one asked.

"You know that old lady you torture by knocking on her door? We're going to fix up her house."

Slade's brothers left in a huff, but we were all agreed on the plan for tomorrow. Of course, they left Slade behind, so Zane and Hunter were helping him hobble home.

Darcy, Fiona, Maya, and I walked slowly through the yard, back toward Maya's house. It was getting late, but we were all abuzz from the night's crazy events.

"I can't believe TDB was a secret society!" Darcy exclaimed. Her eyes glowed with the thrill of it all. "And *we* saved Slade Durkin. I never thought that would happen."

"And Hunter sided with us!" I shook my head in disbelief.

"And *you* figured it out, Norah," Fiona said, giving me a high five.

I didn't want to take all the credit. I'd pieced things together in the end, but there had been a lot of teamwork along the way. Plus, it had all started with one person. I smiled warmly in Maya's direction and said, "None of this would have happened if Maya hadn't been so caring and worried. She came to us with this case when other people might have ignored the sounds."

Maya blushed. "But it was Darcy's idea to charge into the woods and save you."

"That was so awesome!" I said, elbowing Darcy playfully. "How did you know I needed help?" I asked.

Darcy answered, "Fiona, Maya, and I had finished searching all our areas, and you still hadn't come back from the woods. Then Zane and Hunter came outside. They'd been watching together from Hunter's window. They saw you go in the woods from one direction, and then Hunter saw that bouncing light again coming from another direction. They knew someone else was out there — with a flashlight."

"And you guys all banded together to come and find me? So brave!" I pulled the girls together into a giant group hug.

Darcy grinned. "I have to admit, the way we came out from behind the trees counting like that, we totally rocked."

I threw my head back and laughed. "Totally. I have *awesome* friends."

We returned to the living room and finally started to settle down. We crawled over to our sleeping bags and slipped inside. As I lay down, the night replayed in my mind: the voices, the goggles, Slade, his brothers . . . I suddenly felt wiped out. I could hear Fiona's and Maya's steady breathing so I knew they had instantly fallen asleep. But Darcy was still awake.

She reached her hand out of the sleeping bag and aimed her fist at me. "To another solved case!" she whispered.

Smiling, I reached my hand out and bumped her fist. Then I rolled over, feeling warm and proud. But before sleep overtook me, an idea popped into my head.

"Hey, Darcy," I mumbled tiredly, "maybe we could do a sleepover at my house next weekend?"

"Yeah!" Darcy said, sounding happier than I'd heard her in a while.

I closed my eyes and started planning the night. "Fiona could bring her makeup again. And Maya could bring the recipe for those smoothies her mom makes. I was even thinking we could ask Maya to join Partners in Crime. She'd love that."

No sound came from Darcy's sleeping bag.

"Darcy? What do you think?"

There was only silence. She must've fallen asleep.

I fluffed my pillow a bit and got comfortable. Sleep was a good idea. We had a big day of work tomorrow.

Chapter 19

On Sunday, we all descended on Mrs. Wolfson's house. Some of us, out of the goodness of our hearts. The Danville Boys, because they were forced to.

Hunter mowed her weedy lawn. Fiona planted flowers. Zane, Slade, and The Danville Boys got busy scraping the old paint off the porch. They'd all actually shown up, proving that there was hope for everyone. I didn't know for sure how many were in the secret society, but half a dozen came to work, and that was good enough for me.

But Darcy hadn't answered her phone when I called her. She had been the first one up and gone from the sleepover that morning. I left two messages for her, but she still wasn't here.

I carried a can of white paint up the porch steps. It was much heavier than it looked, but I tried not to struggle too much and seem like a total wimp. I put it down next to Zane. "Here's the fresh paint for when you're done scraping," I said. The Danville Boys had even footed the bill for whatever supplies we couldn't scrounge from our garages.

"Thanks," Zane said, smiling. "This was a really nice idea, Norah."

I waved my hand like it was nothing. But on the inside I was jumping up and down. *I impressed Zane!*

But then he frowned for a moment. "Hey, you haven't seen my wallet anywhere, have you? It's black and has a Velcro opening."

I shook my head. "No. Did you lose it today?"

"That's the thing. I must have dropped it somewhere, but I don't remember when I last had it."

Huh. In that case, he might have lost it days ago. "Sorry, Zane. If I find it I'll let you know."

He shrugged. "It's okay. I only had two dollars in there. But it also had my school ID, and now I'll have to get a new one."

Mrs. Wolfson came out with a tray of brownies and yet another pitcher of lemonade. She'd been serving us goodies all morning. She was so happy to see her old house getting spruced up.

"Brownies!" the guys yelled in unison as they barreled up the stairs. That was something they could all agree on — whether they were in a secret society or not.

I went around back to where Maya was pulling weeds from a planting bed.

"How are things with Anya?" I asked her.

She straightened and used her forearm to wipe sweat off her forehead. "The usual. But it's nice to know that she wasn't evil enough to try to purposefully scare me." She smiled bashfully. "And it's nice to know I have real friends now."

I put my hand on her arm. "You do."

I looked around at the pile of weeds she'd pulled. This section would be ready for Fiona to plant flowers into next. "You're doing great here," I said.

Maya smiled. "It feels good to do something nice for Mrs. Wolfson."

"Yeah, it does," I agreed. Especially knowing that, for years, she was ignored and whispered about by kids in the neighborhood. Now she could have a fresh start. Everyone kept telling me how nice I was for organizing this whole thing, but to be honest, it made me just as happy as it made Mrs. Wolfson.

"I'd like to do something nice for you, too," Maya said.

Well, that was unexpected. "Okay . . ."

Maya took a quick look around to make sure no one was coming near us. Then, in a low voice, she said, "I want to tell you Zane's secret."

I had to force myself to swallow. "You shouldn't," I said. "If he wants it kept a secret —"

She waved me toward her and I took a step closer. She whispered, "It's about you, so I think you have a right to know."

Zane's secret is about me? What the —? My heart started pounding like crazy.

Maya's eyes glimmered with delight as she said, "He likes you."

"What?" I squeaked. My lungs seized. I had to remind myself to breathe.

"He *likes* you likes you. He talks about you all the time. But he doesn't really know what to do about it. I told him he should just tell you and that you'll probably like him back, but he's too nervous."

So *that* was what Zane and Maya had been talking about in the hall that day. Me! I felt numb all over. I thought I was going into shock. Wonderful, Best Day Ever shock.

Maya added, "Promise me you'll never let him know I told you."

I brought my finger to my chest and crossed my heart.

Mainly because I couldn't speak.

Zane liked me. What I was going to do with that information, I had no idea. I couldn't act like I knew. Maya had made me promise. But I had to do *something* about it. Zane was right there, in front of Mrs. Wolfson's house, and all I wanted to do was run over and give him a hug, but I was too nervous.

At least I could share the news with my best friend.

I took off from the house, telling everyone that I needed to get another gardening tool, and rode my bike to Darcy's, pedaling harder than I ever had in my life. She'd been teasing me about Zane for so long. It would be great to share this moment together. Even though she'd been moody lately. This crazy news would be just what we needed.

I practically skipped up to her front door and knocked three times. I had to hold in a fit of excited giggles. Finally, the door opened.

Darcy scowled when she saw it was me. "What?"

Not the response I'd been hoping for, but I took a deep breath. I wouldn't let her bad mood ruin this moment for me. I'd put *her* in a good mood instead!

"Can you keep a secret?" I wiggled my fingers excitedly.

Darcy crossed her arms and waited, tapping her foot.

"Maya told me that Zane likes me! Likes me, likes me!" The words burst out of me. It felt so good to say them out loud.

"Wonderful," Darcy snarled. "So now you can go off and be boyfriend-girlfriend with him and ignore me even more."

I froze. My mouth hung open.

Darcy went to close the door and I put my hand up to stop it. "What are you talking about?" I demanded.

She threw her hands up in the air. "You have no time for me anymore. We *used* to be best friends."

I stood stunned for a moment. "We *are* best friends. You'll always be my best friend. What's wrong with you?"

"What's wrong with *you*?" she snapped back. "We used to spend every afternoon together. Now you're bringing all these new people into our group."

I didn't understand what was going on. Why was she so mad? I swallowed a giant lump in my throat. "But you like Fiona. We *both* agreed to bring her into our group."

"That was before her opinion became more important than mine."

"What do you mean?" I sputtered. I told myself not to cry.

Darcy's eyes flashed. "You didn't believe me when I said your glasses looked cool, but you believed her. And you went house to house with her, investigating, rather than wait one day for me to do it with you. It's like you're forgetting about me."

"It's . . . it's . . . not like that," I stammered.

"And you even started dressing like her and *lying* to me to spend time with her." Darcy's voice shook with anger.

I staggered back a step. "What?"

Darcy pointed at me. "I saw you. Wednesday when you said you were too busy to watch *Crime Scene: New York* with me, Fiona went into your house with you and was there forever."

Oh no. I'd only meant for Fiona to stay a few minutes. I hadn't planned on her staying for Family Movie Night. I'd hurt Darcy's feelings without even realizing it. No wonder she'd seemed different the last few days.

"Wait," I said. "I can explain."

"With more lies?" She rolled her eyes. "I don't think so."

My throat tightened. "We can fix this," I said. "We just need to talk it —"

Darcy interrupted, "Last night when you asked me to sleep over at your house next weekend, I thought, 'Great! I'm finally going to have my best friend all to myself again. Even if just for one night.' But then you started rattling off all the things Fiona and Maya could bring. And then I found out you'd already decided to have Maya join Partners in Crime!"

It all sounded so terrible the way Darcy was saying it, but I truly never meant to hurt her. If I'd known she wanted some time with just us, I would have totally done it. But she never told me! I opened my mouth to explain, but she snapped, "So go have fun with all your new friends and your new boyfriend."

I felt sick. She wasn't even letting me talk. How was I supposed to tell my side of the story? I lashed out, "Well, maybe I don't appreciate that you always assume the worst in people. Including me."

Red colored her cheeks and she raised her voice. "I'm sick of how nice you always have to be to everyone."

"And I'm sick of how moody you are!" I snapped back.

Darcy tilted her chin up. "Then maybe we shouldn't be best friends anymore."

No!

That wasn't what I wanted. Not at all. But I was so angry at the way she was acting. Before I could stop the words from escaping, I said, "Maybe not."

Darcy set her jaw and took a step back from me. "Fine, then. We're over."

I felt a squeezing in my chest. Actual physical pain. Darcy slammed the door, but I still heard her last words from the other side.

"And so is Partners in Crime."

I spent the next few hours crying in bed. Hubble jumped on the blanket and curled up beside me. He always seemed to know when I was sad. But even petting him and looking into his cute little dog face wasn't making this better.

Darcy and I had been friends forever, so of course we'd had arguments before. But this one felt different. And that scared me.

It had always been just Darcy and me since fourth grade. That never bothered me, but I'd enjoyed making new friends like Fiona and Maya. I never realized that I'd made Darcy feel like I was leaving her behind. And, just like our case with Abigail and Trey, this could've all been avoided if Darcy had been honest about her feelings. She should've told me sooner.

The truth was that, while I liked Fiona and Maya, neither of them compared to Darcy. She knew me in a way only my family did. No one could ever take her place.

But I might have ruined everything.

How could I fix the mess we were in? This was a mystery I hoped I could solve. And soon.

Don't miss Norah and Darcy's next case!

sleuth or dare

#3: Framed & Dangerous

I snuck up to Mr. Plati's door. I couldn't make out the words he was saying, but it was clear that he was using his angry voice. It wasn't exactly yelling, but it was loud enough that I could quietly push the door open an inch and he wouldn't notice.

"And you're sure you had nothing to do with the fire?" Mr. Plati was asking Zane skeptically.

My heart sped up.

"Yes, sir," Zane answered with a tremble in his voice. "You know me. I've never been in trouble before. I would never do something like this."

There was a long pause. I wished I could put my eye up to the crack to see their expressions. Why didn't Mr. Plati believe Zane? Of course he had nothing to do with the fire. My chest squeezed.

"We have a problem, then, Mr. Munro."

"What is it?" Zane asked.

I felt so bad for him, facing this all alone in there. Why would anyone want to put Zane through this?

Mr. Plati let out a long sigh, like he was deeply disappointed. "The problem is that, in addition to setting the fire, you've also now lied to me. Because I know you were at the field house. I have evidence."

My mind scrambled. Evidence? What evidence?

I heard the squeak of a drawer opening. And the light thud of something being placed on the desk. Then I heard Zane gasp.

I couldn't take it anymore. I risked it and put my eye up to the crack.

"This was found at the scene of the crime," Mr. Plati said. "Look familiar?"

He lifted a small black item in his hand. A wallet. Zane's wallet.

I rocked back on my heels like I'd been slapped. Whoever set the fire had stolen Zane's wallet or found it after he'd dropped it. Then they put it at the scene to frame him. I was overcome with anger. My face felt like it was burning.

"Are you going to deny that this is your wallet?" Mr. Plati asked. "Because your student ID is inside."

Zane paled. "No, I mean, yes, that's my wallet. But I lost that a few days ago."

Mr. Plati raised his eyebrows. "Inside the field house?"

Zane shook his head. "No. I've never been in the field house. It wasn't open yet."

"But when Mr. Gray ran in to try to stop the fire" — Mr. Plati pointed a finger at the wallet — "he found this on the floor."

"I — I — I," Zane stuttered.

I'd never heard him this nervous. My heart went out to him.

"Someone's framing me!" he blurted. "I got a threatening e-mail and everything!"

Mr. Plati leaned forward on his desk and clasped his hands. "Is that really the tactic you're going to use?"

"It's the truth," Zane said, bewildered. "Why would I burn the field house?"

Mr. Plati let out an aggravated grunt. "I overheard a conversation in the hall last week, between the soccer team and the basketball team. It seems some of you boys on the soccer team were all riled up about the field house."

Zane's face turned bright red, and he looked down at the floor. "We're just mad because the basketball team gets a brand-new field house and we're basically kicked out. We used to practice here and now we have to go all the way to the high school for practices. It's not fair."

Mr. Plati nodded. "I heard that. It would've been hard not to, since you were using such a raised voice."

"We were angry," Zane muttered.

"But how angry?" Mr. Plati asked quietly. "Angry enough to 'burn the field house down?'" He used finger quotes as he said the words.

I nearly slid down to the floor in shock. He was *quoting* Zane? Zane *threatened* to burn the field house down?

Zane's shoulders shook. "I was only joking when I said that. It was just one of those things you say but you don't mean."

"That's what I assumed at the time," the principal said. "I thought to myself, 'Zane Munro is a good kid. He's angry right now and that's why these words are flying, but he certainly doesn't want the field house to burn down.'" He shifted in his seat. "But the problem is, Mr. Munro, that the field house *did* burn down. A week after you said that. And your wallet was found at the scene." He took a long pause. "Are you sure there's nothing you need to tell me?"

Zane's eyes were glassy. "No, sir."

Mr. Plati leaned back in his chair and pinched the bridge of his nose. "I'm disappointed in you, Zane. I hoped that you'd be honest and face what you did. You're better than this."

Zane banged his hand on the arm of the chair. "I didn't do it, Principal Plati. I swear! Someone is framing me!"

But Mr. Plati only shook his head. "I've already called your parents. They're on their way. The police will be taking over from now on. You can show this supposed e-mail to them. In the meantime, you're suspended from school and banned from school events. No soccer games. No dance."

My heart broke into a thousand pieces. Only a few minutes ago, it had seemed like Zane was going to ask me to my first dance. I'd been so excited and had so much to look forward to. And now it was all falling apart.

In a deep, sorrowful tone, Mr. Plati ended with, "And the rest depends on the results of the investigation."

I scurried back into the hall. Zane emerged from the office a moment later, looking stricken.

"I heard everything," I whispered.

Zane looked up at me with eyes that held no hope. "You believe me, right? I did say that about the field house, but only because I was mad. I didn't mean it. I never, ever would have done something like this."

I put my hand on his shoulder and said firmly, "I believe you. I know you didn't do this."

Zane's shoulders sagged. "I'm in huge trouble, Norah. I'm suspended and I might even get charged with a crime."

I clenched my fists. Not if I had anything to do with it.

POISON APPLE BOOKS

The Dead End

This Totally Bites!

Miss Fortune

Now You See Me...

Midnight Howl

Her Evil Twin

Curiosity Killed the Cat

At First Bite

THRILLING.
BONE-CHILLING.
THESE BOOKS
HAVE BITE!

YOU NEVER KNOW WHAT WILL HAPPEN TOMORROW

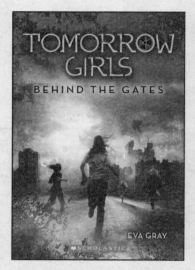

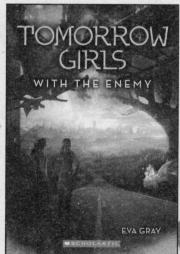

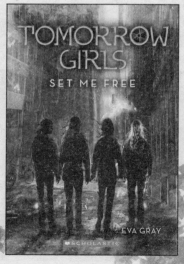